THE RED HAIRED WOMAN
AND OTHER STORIES

The Red-Haired Woman
and other stories

By
SIGERSON CLIFFORD

Introduction by
BRENDAN KENNELLY

THE MERCIER PRESS
CORK AND DUBLIN

The Mercier Press Limited
4 Bridge Street, Cork
24 Lower Abbey Street, Dublin 1

ISBN 0 85342 882 4

Many of these stories first appeared in The Irish Press, The Evening Press *and* The Kerryman.

The characters and situations in this book are entirely imaginary and bear no relation to any real person or actual happening. Any resemblance to real persons, living or dead, is purely coincidental.

Printed by Litho Press Co., Midleton, Co. Cork.

Contents

Preface

In remembering past times I remember most my husband's strong love for his native place. Every year as July edged nearer August he became restless. As evening came on he was out in the back-garden carefully examining the night sky for signs of good weather. Then one night he would say, 'I'll be off so in the morning' and thus the annual visit to Cahirciveen, Co. Kerry, would begin.

Like the Scholar-Gypsy, rumoured sightings of him came back to us. He was seen in the early morning going up the Rocky Road, walking stick in hand, on his way to his favourite haunts and once, an old friend was amazed to come across him in some quiet place, sitting on a large stone in midstream, paddling his feet in the running water. But the visit to Cahirciveen lasted at most three to four days and he was back to us again, smiling and at peace with the world, like a pilgrim returning from a holy place, and content to remain in his Dublin back-garden for the rest of the summer.

In January, 1985, on a day of snow and ice, we took him back to Cahirciveen for the last time.

The following are some of the stories he left behind.

Marie Clifford

INTRODUCTION

When I was putting together *The Penguin Book of Irish Verse* I wrote to Sigerson Clifford for permission to include a ballad from his splendid collection, *Ballads of a Bogman.* He replied, giving me permission and suggesting we meet. We did and I was taken immediately by the sight of this big, likeable man whose conversation was full of stories and memories of his boyhood in South Kerry. Shy at first, he soon opened up and the talk flowed out of him.

He loved poetry. I asked him about his ballads and in his reply he emphasised that Eamon Keane, the well-known actor from Listowel, was the person who recited his ballads with the deepest kind of passionate understanding. I agreed.

I have been reading Sigerson Clifford's short stories. The first thing I would say about them is that they are indeed short, some being only two or three pages long. But brevity is not only the soul of wit; it is, in the case of Sigerson Clifford, the mark of a talented storyteller. His stories open crisply, proceed vigorously and conclude surprisingly or quietly or even, at times, predictably. Short as they are, however, several linger in my memory.

The language of these stories is bright and lively. And those who are aware of Clifford's gifts as a playwright will not be surprised to find that many of the pieces have a strongly dramatic character and contain sharp and pointed dialogue. He can create a dramatic atmosphere with a few deft, telling strokes. As well as that, he can bring his characters alive in a few brief sentences. He writes like a man who has a deep, intimate knowledge of the people who fill his stories; nothing is strained or unnatural; the stories move easily and fluently. They grow out of the oral tradition which is also the source and inspiration of Clifford's remarkable ballads.

This collection of stories has humour, shrewd observation, sharp wit at times, and the calm, sure touch of the accomplished storyteller. Naturally, readers will prefer some stories to others; but there's enough variety in this book, brief though the stories be, to please most people. You will remember *The Red-Haired Woman, Master Melody, The Spanish Waistcoat, The Rebel* and *Randal's Ring* long after you've forgotten the big, blaring headlines that assault your eyes contemplating the morning paper. Long may you enjoy the reading and re-reading of these delightful little stories.

Brendan Kennelly

1. The Red-Haired Woman

All that morning the Fair Green had been a bedlam of lowing cattle, barking dogs and shouting men keeping their beasts herded together with whacking ashplants. Now it was empty save for the county council's unbroken stones in the centre, the tarred electric-light pole, with a circus poster wrapped around it, at the top, and James Moylan with his bullock standing mournfully beside the school wall at the bottom.

He was a small man with sad blue eyes and bushy eyebrows so fiercely red one looked at them and almost forgot to notice his eyes. He was extremely thin and his clothes hung loosely about him as though someone had pitched them carelessly upon him with a hay-fork. He wore a chequered tweed cap with a high crown down on his forehead.

The bullock was also very thin. He was a black yearling with the brown patient eyes of his kind. No amount of feeding could fatten him. His black unhealthy hide was stretched very tightly about him so that his backbone and ribs made ridges in it. He was like a slim upturned canvas-canoe on legs.

Moylan raised his stick and cut the beast across its lean flank.

'Go along, you brute,' he said.

There was a little bubble of anger in him at not making a sale. His brother had sold four heifers while you'd be cracking an egg. Fifteen pounds a skull he got for them. His brother's wife and his own were sisters. They both had tongues as sharp as a cobbler's awl. As he remembered that, he hit the bullock again. She'd stitch him up with abuse when he got home with the beast still unsold.

He blamed Red Ellie for his failure to sell. She stood before him on the road that morning, shook her splendid mane of foxy hair at him, and laughed. He should have returned to his house straightaway and waited 'till she left the road. It was what the fishermen always did when they met her. It meant bad luck to meet a red-haired woman when you went fishing or selling. Everyone knew that.

Red Ellie was a widow who owned the mountainy farm next to him. She was a stout roomy woman with blue patches like maps on the calves of her legs. Some special herb grew on her piece of the mountain and his sheep were forever going there in search of it. She had summonsed him for trespass scores of times, the Justice only fining him small amounts because he was sick of the woman's pettiness.

'Have you any solution, Moylan, for this childish bickering?' the Justice asked him once.

He twisted his cap in his hands but the porter in him gave him courage.

'The only way out, sir —'. He paused to think.

'Yes, Moylan, go on,' encouraged the Justice.

'Would be to poison the wife, your honour, and marry the widow,' he suggested.

The court laughed so loud that it frightened him and Red Ellie hated him more than ever.

As he thought on the woman the bubble within him burst and he struck his stick against the school wall three or four times.

'God's curse on you, Red Ellie,' he cried. 'May the flagstones of hell blister your heels for eternity.'

He felt better for a prayer like that and his anger subsided. He stood at ease waving his stick gently from side to side, wondering what he should do. Then he saw Dwyer, the jobber, coming across the Green towards him and his heart jumped. He took out his pipe and began to scrape the bowl with a knife as though the jobber's arrival did not concern him in the least.

'Be damn, James, I could hardly see you with the crowd,' said Dwyer. He struck his gaitered calf with a yellow cane and laughed. He had the loud, fat laugh of a man who always eats a good meal and has a roll of notes in his inside pocket to pay for it.

'Where's your brother, Michael?' asked the jobber.

'He's accustomed to go to Carey's, Mr Dwyer,' said James. 'You'll likely find him there.'

'There's no better judge of cattle in the country than Michael,' declared Dwyer. He let his eye run over the bullock's bony frame.

'He wants fattening, Mr Dwyer,' said James.

'All the corn in Egypt wouldn't put another pick on him,' decided the jobber. He looked pityingly at the beast's protruding ribs. 'He's only fit for the one thing, James. Take him out to sea, stand him on a rock, and put a burning candle inside him, and he'll make a first class light-house.'

He walked away, laughing loudly. He shouted back over his shoulder, 'Carey's you said, James?'

James, silently, watched him 'till he turned the corner of the school wall.

The bullock began to bellow, his whole thin body heaving with the strain of making sound, until James thought he'd collapse at his feet. The sound irritated him just as the thought of his shrewish wife and Red Ellie annoyed him a few minutes before. He struck the beast sharply on its ballooning neck.

'The devil bellow you,' he said.

The bullock leaped forward, his tail curved in an arc. He ran towards the opening in the top right-hand corner of the Green that began the road leading to the west. James followed him, belabouring him with the stick until he galloped out of range.

'Clear home out of this, you brat,' he shouted as though it were a cross child playing tricks on him. 'Clear home to hell out of this.'

The bullock went bellowing through the Green gap and disappeared.

When he went into Carey's public house it was packed with people. Farmers filled the front of the shop, leaning against the bar counter or sitting at the smaller counter opposite it as they drank and talked. At the back of the shop six town youths sat on a stool, their glasses balanced on their knees, or placed carefully between their ankles on the floor. They came there every fair day to sing racy ballads and listen to the farmers talking. They considered themselves superior to the people living on the land and referred to them as the country boys. The farmers had a profound contempt for the townies and carefully noted everything they said and did for future mimicking at the cross-roads debating schools.

He saw his brother, Michael, at the counter and he went up to him.

'I didn't sell,' he said, dully

'I'd be surprised if you did,' answered his brother. 'They don't employ blind men as cattle-jobbers these days.'

James nodded. 'Dwyer was looking for you.' It was more a question than a statement.

'I saw him,' said Michael. 'He wants me to buy cattle for him. Good cattle.'

'He knows your worth,' approved James, satisfied with the information. He drew the back of his hand across his stubby chin. 'I have no money on me,' he said.

His brother gave him a pound.

'Will you have a drink, Michael?'

'I'm in company,' said Michael.

He realised that his brother was angry with him for bringing the bullock to the fair, and didn't want to drink with him.

'Nothing could fatten him. Nothing. He has a serpent inside him and it swallows all he ates,' he excused himself. His brother said nothing but dug his nose in his pint.

He moved up the shop and stood opposite the townies. He ordered a pint and the girl filled it for him. She had red hair, too, and he stared at it with inimical eyes.

'Did you sell, James?' she asked.

'No,' he said, 'I met a foxy woman on the road.'

'You couldn't have luck,' she teased him. 'And foxy women as plentiful as crows in the land!'

He raised the glass and drank keenly. Then he smacked his lips loudly and shuddered at the cold feel of the drink in his stomach. A farmer beside him, a stranger to him, nodded at the half empty glass.

'Begor, you put a hole in it that time,' he said admiringly.

'Ah, 'tis wake stuff,' James deprecated. 'It's not what it was. I remember a time you had eating and drinking in it, 'twas that strong.'

'We'll have good times again, please God,' promised the stranger.

'Please God,' said James. He dashed off the remainder of his drink.

'What'll you have?' he asked.

They drank and conversed happily together until James was drunk and Bid Mara the tinker came in, her left arm hooked about a basket containing lace, cards of safety-pins, studs and cheap ties.

She was a tall, splendidly built woman with cruel blue eyes. She had a head of glowing, carefully-combed, golden hair falling into a knot at the nape of her neck. Her face now bloated and discoloured from too much intoxication still showed traces of its former youthful handsomeness. She was forty years of age.

James turned and saw her. He nudged his companion.

'She's like a dragoon,' he said.

He leaned against the counter and watched her in mouth-wide admiration. She approached and stood looking down at him, sizing him up. She caught his hand in hers and began to squint at the palm.

'Will I show you the future, good sir, will I tell you your fortune?' she chanted.

He regarded her silently a few moments.

'Tell me the past,' he said heavily, 'so as I'll know if you're a liar.'

'I'll tell the decent gentleman what's in store for him so,' she evaded.

He was conscious of everyone's eyes upon him and he thrust out his chin.

'The past or nothing,' he shouted, 'Ye can all tell the future but have ye a knowledge of the past?'

He held up half-a-crown.

'I'll give you this bar of silver if you tell me my past.'

He grinned broadly at her, knowing he had her beaten, feeling that the crowded house thought him a clever man to get the best of her like that. He expanded his chest, nodding his head delightedly and winked at the six townies who were watching the entertainment with amused eyes. He twirled the half-crown about on his finger tips mocking her. Suddenly, like a frog's tongue licking up a fly, her hand whipped the coin from his fingers and slipped it into her mouth.

He stood staring foolishly at her until somebody laughed and goaded him to action. He leaned forward and caught her shawl in his fist. He began to shout, 'Give me back that piece of silver or by the gates of heaven —'

Before he could finish it she struck him under the right eye with her clenched fist and knocked him down. He lay on his back looking up dazedly at her through a Christmas tree of stars. Then the enormous indignity of it piled into his brain and he got to his feet with a roar. He sprang at her but the men held him by the shoulders.

'Let me at her,' he shouted. 'Let me get my two bare hands on the tinker hag.'

He began to rear and curvet like a colt on its first rope but they were too strong for him. Two of the other men shoved Bid Mara into the street.

When she was gone he quietened down. He turned to the men that held him.

'Ye shouldn't have weighed me down, he told them. 'She'll do the likes to someone else if she's not chastised.'

He looked at his drinking companion.

'I bested her anyway,' he boasted, 'she couldn't read the past.'

'You did. You bested her,' agreed his friend, watching the dark patch spreading under his bloodshot eye. "Twas a clever thought to make her read the past.'

His brother, Michael, who had watched the whole occurrence in silent rage and mortification could contain himself no longer. He rushed forward and caught James by the throat.

'You drunken fool,' he cried, 'making a circus of yourself before the scum of the town.'

The town boys groaned audibly in mock resentment.

'Why were you up-and-down with her likes at all?' asked Michael. 'She's not your class.'

James rocked back on his heels. He was tired, hungry and sore, and he wanted to sleep. He liked his brother and was sorry he had hurt his pride.

'It's all right, Michael,' he soothed, 'I'm going home now.'

He went out of the public house and walked until he had left the town behind him. He came to a meadow and stood a while looking at it. The sun was warm and a haze of heat hung above the glinting cocks. He climbed the gate and went in. He lay down in the shade of the nearest cock and fell asleep.

It was dark when he awoke and hit the road for home again. The lump under his eye was throbbing and it hurt when he fingered it. He walked on revolving the memories of the day in his mind, and cursing Red Ellie.

Half a mile from his own door he saw the bullock grazing by the side of the road. He drove the beast before him, slapping him gently with his stick. He felt sorry for the rough way he had treated the brute in the morning.

'How could I sell you,' he said 'and a foxy witch living up to my elbow, putting her evil spells upon me?'

When he came to Red Ellie's house she was asleep. There was no light there and the corrugated-iron was silvered by the stars. He stopped and looked and his eye began to throb fiercely. He shook his stick at the sleeping house and worked himself into a rage against his persecutor.

'If ever you stand before me on the road again, Red Ellie, I'll cut your throat,' he shouted. 'D'you hear? D'you hear?'

There was a pile of stones beside the road. He flung them on the iron roof as fast as he could throw them until his arm tired of it. The stones fell with the noise of exploding bombs, filling the night with indecent sound.

He felt better then and his eye stopped paining him. He was conscious of having accomplished something to balance the many injustices she had done him. He walked in a lively fashion up the road, away from Red Ellie's battered house. He sang as he walked....

2. The Spanish Waistcoat

John Dan's house looked upon Kersey village, and Kersey looked on the sea. It was a small, neat house with walls white as fresh milk and laced by wires anchored to heavy stones to keep the thatch from flying over the mountain when the great winds blew from the sea. John Dan lived alone in the house.

He was a tall, clumsy man, high over sixty, with huge hairy hands and the biggest pair of boots in the parish. He smoked a pipe continuously. It was a stubby evil-smelling briar and it bubbled furiously when smoked. In the chapel on Sundays people avoided kneeling beside John Dan because the pipe, tucked carefully at the bottom of his coat-pocket, was no less offensive to the nose than if it had been gripped between the last four decaying teeth in the left corner of John Dan's mouth. That's the kind of pipe it was.

One fine midday John Dan, smoking and bubbling merrily against his western gable, saw a knot of people leave the wide road and walk urgently up the boreen towards him. He recognised Murthy the Post by reason of his dark blue uniform, with the polished brass buttons winking on it like little yellow eyes, and the glossy peak of his cap flashing like a mirror in the sun. 'There's strangeness here,' said John Dan to himself, and he waited and wondered.

The only time in the year Murthy called to a house so far removed from the main road as John Dan's was at Christmas, when he got a half-crown and a drop of whiskey to tide him over till that bountiful season came again. At all other times he stopped on the wide road, draped himself across his bicycle, whistled shrilly three times and waited patiently until the house disgorged somebody to collect the letter. So it was strange indeed to see him straining his heart climbing the mountain in the high heat of noon, when three shrill whistles would have brought John Dan down to the wide road to gather his mail. And Christmas so far off, and all.

As they drew nearer John Dan saw a parcel in Murthy's hand. 'Maybe 'tis a case of pipes from Nora,' he told himself.

John Dan had two daughters in America, and a brother, Denny, living ten miles across the Sound in Beglin. Nora, who was married to an Italian café owner, often sent him a few dollars. She also posted him the money to buy the green punt from Michael John Shea when he decided to take one of the farms in County Meath that the government were giving to mountainy people. The little boat was handy to John Dan for the bit of pollack-fishing he did, and it enabled him to keep his eye on the dozen lobster-pots he had anchored in his own special patch of sea beyond Lamb's Point. His other daughter, Gobnait, still unmarried and, in John Dan's opinion, likely to remain so, never sent anything except highly-coloured Christmas cards plastered with highly-coloured sentiments and signed: 'To dearest Pop from Netta.' One year in America had taught Gobnait to change John Dan's name and her own in one fell swoop....

He went across the yard to meet the men, his eyes curious.

''Tis from America,' said Murthy, giving him the parcel, 'and there's twenty-five shillings tax on it.'

'May the devil sweep 'em with their twenty-five shillings tax,' fumed John Dan, turning the parcel over in his hands. He carefully read the labels attached to the parcel.

''Tis wearing apparel,' he told the crowd, 'and, be the hokey, 'tis from Gobnait.'

'We know that,' said Paddy the Black Bog honestly and easily. 'We only want to see what's in it.'

''Tisn't every day you pay twenty-five shillings tax on a biteen of a garment,' said William Red Sails. 'There must be powerful stuff in it.'

They all went into the house and John Dan sawed the cords asunder with a gapped bread-knife. He unwound enough tissue-paper to make a sail for a boat and then the garment in all its glory lay before them.

It was a curious piece of work, to say the least of it. It was more like a waistcoat than a coat only it had long sleeves. It was beautifully embroidered in gold and silver with a buffalo grazing on the left breast and a puma snarling on the right.

'What devil's curio is this?' asked John Dan, turning a bewildered eye on Murthy, who was feeling quite bewildered himself.

'Let me see now,' said Murthy, fingering the garment while the others waited expectantly for his decision.

Before he graduated into a whistling postman, Murthy had been a sailor. He had crossed the line, rounded Cape Horn, had been shipwrecked a few times and had had a knife stuck into him by an unfriendly Arab in a brawl in Cairo. In consequence of these varied and almost disastrous experiences Murthy's words carried some weight in the parish of Kersey.

Murthy examined the garment inside and out and felt his pedestal trembling for a fall beneath him.

'If Murthy doesn't know, nobody knows,' said John Dan earnestly to Paddy Black Bog, 'and him after ringing the world a score of times.'

Murthy's eyes gleamed and his words came slow and ponderous like well-fed cows through a gap in a drowsy June dusk.

'I seen the likes of it in Spain. The bull-fighters in Madrid used to wear its equal. 'Tis a Spanish waistcoat.'

The others emitted their breath in little whistles of appreciation and fingered the waistcoat with renewed interest. There was no country in the world so near to the minds of the people of Kersey as Spain. They knew their history and were well aware that she sent them ships round about 1600 which is only the day before yesterday to a

Kersey man. And wasn't she still sending ships? To be sure the great gilded galleons had now become swift, well-designed, if ill-designing, trawlers which left their fishing-grounds as bare as the palm of your hand, but they were still ships and showed that Spain had not forgotten them entirely. So one can imagine the tidal wave of excitement that swept over John Dan's house when it was revealed by the wise Murthy that the richly-embroidered garment was nothing less than a Spanish waistcoat as worn by the bull-fighters of Spain who are, as every mother's son should know, the real aristocracy of that orange-blessed land.

Paddy Black Bog smote John Dan heartily between the shoulder-blades. 'You'll dazzle the parish with this,' said Paddy. 'I can see you sitting snug in the Widow Breheny's place a month from today.'

William Red Sails winced visibly at the dire prophecy. William, who was, fortunately in the circumstances, a widower, had an interest in the Widow himself and had dreamed dreams and seen visions. And the Widow had twenty acres of the best land in Kersey and a black box which she always kept locked. Locked black boxes in any other part of Ireland are not as intriguing as those in Kersey. For in Kersey a locked black box means that its owner does not appreciate the fact that banks are run at enormous expense for the sole purpose of helping those who deem it necessary to get a lock for a black box. And William Red Sails never counted John Dan much of a rival. But now all was changed, changed utterly.

'You'll wear the Spanish waistcoat on Sunday going to Mass,' commanded Paddy Black Bog, 'and I'll speak a few words to the Widow about you in the meantime.'

'Is it a grey or a black trousers I'll wear with it?' asked John Dan.

''Tis a red trousers they used wear in Madrid,' said Murthy, scratching his chin. 'But, of course, Kersey isn't Madrid,' he confided, 'and you could wear the black.'

'The black it is,' said John Dan.

On Saturday John Dan walked into Kersey and looked in on Jackie Walsh, the draper.

'I'm after a good hat, Jackie,' he said.

'How good?' asked Jackie.

'One fit to go with my Spanish waistcoat,' said John Dan proudly.

On Sunday morning all Kersey collected at the western end of the village to await the triumphant entry of John Dan. The fame of the Spanish waistcoat had gone through the parish with the speed of a mackerel-shoal evading the nets of a fishing-boat down to its last tin of condensed milk. The Widow Breheny was there, too, her fifteen stone swathed in a fur coat that had cost her a pony, though the shop assistant in Tralee town assured her 'twas a squirrel had worn it before her, and sporting a hat whose twin was never beheld on land or sea.

At last John Dan arrived, guarded on either side by Murthy the Post and Paddy Black Bog. He was coatless and the Spanish waistcoat, wooed by an appreciating sun, sparkled like the toga of an archangel. He wore his new black hat at an angle that lifted ten years off his total of three score and seven, and the crease on his trousers was razor-sharp. His face had the frightened exalted look of a man, wrongly condemned, on his way to the guillotine, in sharp contrast to the countenances of his benevolent executioners, Murthy and Paddy, which were wreathed in smiles.

A hush fell on the villagers and on the Widow Breheny's fur coat and the eyes of the multitude watched with mingled awe and admiration the progress of the new John Dan. Caesar entering Rome after dividing all Gaul into three parts didn't command half as much respect as John Dan did in his triumphant Spanish-waistcoated entry into Kersey.

The three men were half-way down the line before somebody thought of raising a cheer. In a moment it had swelled to a mighty roar that shook the windows of Kersey and gave the wondering collectors at the chapel some inkling as to why their boxes were still bare of pennies.

Father Dermot, affectionately contemplating his bed of prize red wallflowers and thinking how much they resembled little children dressed in old-fashioned velvet dresses, heard the cheering and lifted his head to find John Dan and all his parishioners bearing down on him.

'Bless my soul,' exclaimed Father Dermot when the luxuriance of John Dan's waistcoat impressed itself upon him. He turned to Paddy Black Bog.

'Is there a name for this — ?' he waved his hand feebly in the direction of John Dan's embroidered chest.

'It's a Spanish waistcoat, Father,' explained Paddy. "Twas worn by a bullfighter in Madrid.'

'A bullfighter. Bless my soul,' said Father Dermot. 'Well, well, let ye march into Mass now. 'Tis getting late.' He watched them till they disappeared through the wide door.

'Bless my soul!' he exclaimed again. 'A bullfighter in Kersey! What will they think of next?'

In the parish of Kersey and indeed beyond it, John Dan's name was on everybody's lips. People who had formerly barely tolerated him now engaged him in lengthy conversations and got his opinions on the correct way to rear bonhams, catch lobsters, where the best fishing grounds for pollack were, and how to divine water with the help of a hazel-rod. They remembered the doughty deeds of his youth, his great skill as a weight-thrower, his prowess on the football field and as an oarsman.

John Dan's suit with the Widow Breheny was being pressed assiduously by Paddy Black Bog. Because of his great, though new-found, fame, one would imagine it to be roses, roses all the way for him, but the Widow wasn't young any longer, and William Red Sails owned the best fishing-boat in the harbour. So she decided to wait a while, and Paddy conveyed the news to John Dan.

'The ould wreck is putting it on the long finger, but I'll bate her into it yet.'

It was unfortunate that the fame of the Spanish waistcoat crossed the ten miles of sea to John Dan's brother, Denny, who was married in Beglin. He wrote to John Dan, inviting him over for a weekend, with a PS not to forget the famous waistcoat.

John Dan decided to go. He went down to the pier one evening when it was dusk and found a boatload of the young bucks setting out for Beglin with a box of lobsters, there being a better price offered in that village than in Kersey.

'Are you coming with us, John Dan?' called out Billy, son to William Red Sails, a lean stringy youth, who was eyeing the Spanish waistcoat as a weasel might eye a month-old rabbit.

They fussed around him, half of them hindering, and the rest helping him into the boat.

'Make way there for the grand Spanish gentleman,' they shouted with unholy glee.

John Dan took the tiller and they pushed off.

'Let ye go by Lamb's Point, boys, I want to haul my pots and bring a few lobsters to Denny,' said John Dan.

'Lamb's Point it is, captain,' they chorused, and their six oars rose and fell cleanly like knife blades.

John Dan ran his experienced eye from stroke to bow.

'Bow oar, pick-up,' he called out.

Billy Red Sails held up his right hand.

'It's my wrist, John Dan, I hurt it this morning hauling the pots.'

John Dan took off his Spanish waistcoat, folded it carefully, and placed it on the stern.

'There's no sense in sending a boy on a man's errand,' he said. 'Give me the oar.'

'Give the Spanish gentleman the oar,' the bloods shouted. 'Get astern, Red Sails, and mind the gentleman's waistcoat.'

The boat leaped forwards again, the oars biting triangles of phosphorescent fire out of the heaving breast of the sea. Soon they were at Lamb's Point and while John Dan rested the others crowded about the stern, hauling his pots and shouting loudly when one contained a lobster.

'Here's one, John Dan, with tusks on him like an elephant.'

'Here's a fellow must be drawing a pension. Give him a shaugh of the pipe, John Dan.'

'This chap has a face on him like a head-constable.'

'Rogues and blackguards,' murmured John Dan. 'I wonder is every parish cursed with the likes of ye?'

They sunk the pots again, sat under their oars and pulled quickly to where the village of Beglin huddled about its score of lights. When they glided into the harbour the pier was deserted. They stood up in the boat and stretched their cramped legs. John Dan made his way to the stern while they were arguing as to who should carry the box of lobsters to the buyer. He put his hand down on the stern-seat and felt along it. Nothing but wood, wet in parts where the sea had spilled on it. He felt again to make sure. No sign of it. A dreadful fear gripped him. He cracked a match, cupped it in his hands, and flashed it on the bottom of the boat. He saw his own three lobsters watching him coldly, their long black feelers waving briskly, and a baling-tin carrying an advertisement for somebody's cream toffees. There was no trace of the Spanish waistcoat.

He turned on the crew in a rage.

'What did ye do with it, ye limbs of Satan? Where did ye put my waistcoat?'

They looked at him open-mouthed.

'He lost the Spanish waistcoat.'

'Find it for him; he'll freeze in his shirt.'

'We'll keel-haul the man that took it.'

''Tis overboard it went. Some mermaid is decking herself out in it now.'

They cracked a score of jokes and matches and searched the boat from stem to stern but there was no sign of it.

They went up on the pier carrying their box of lobsters and John Dan remained in the boat.

'Aren't you going to visit Denny, John Dan?' they asked.

'How can a decent Christian walk through a strange village in his shirt?' said John Dan.

They went along the pier, loudly discussing the mysterious disappearance of the Spanish waistcoat, and vanished into the night.

John Dan wrapped himself in a piece of sail and sat in the stern. He decided to fill his pipe and then remembered that his plug of tobacco was in the pocket of the waistcoat. He grunted loudly. He felt lost and lonely and cold.

'Would to God,' sorrowed John Dan to himself. 'Would to God, we had died in Egypt!'

With the disappearance of the Spanish waistcoat John Dan's fall from glory was swifter than his rise to it. Paddy Black Bog washed his hands of his matrimonial affairs and the Widow Breheny was married to William Red Sails within a month. However, the Widow gave William such a time of it, that he was able to repent at leisure the haste and extreme indiscretion of his second voyage into matrimonial waters. Murthy the Post whistled John Dan down to the wide road whenever he had a letter for him, and never mentioned the waistcoat any more.

John Dan took his loss hard. It was a fortnight before he ventured into Kersey village. It was a month before he decided to visit his lobster-pots.

He rowed out to them in the green punt, his pipe rising poisonous clouds in the still evening air and gurgling like a June turkey. He hauled up eleven of the pots, found them empty, baited them and let them slide down to the green depths again. The twelfth pot was heavy and he knew it had something in it.

'Must be a devil of a conger,' muttered John Dan, opening his big pocket-knife and placing it beside him.

When the pot came to the surface his eyes goggled. There, nestling among the thin rods was his Spanish waistcoat, its grand embroidery ruined for ever, with a big patch of slime whitening where a conger-eel had slept on it.

John Dan drew forth the shabby sodden garment tenderly and looked at it thoughtfully. He felt in the pocket and pulled out the plug of tobacco. He then flung the Spanish waistcoat back into the sea. It floated a while and slipped slowly to the bottom. John Dan watched it wistfully till it disappeared.

3. My South Kerry Grandfathers

When Hallowe'en comes I always remember my grandfather. My mother's father he was, a small bright-eyed little man, five feet or so, and as warm-hearted as toast from the fire. I liked him for the great bag of stories he had, and also, for the penny he gave me every Friday when he drew the pension. You'd get twelve toffees for a penny then from Mrs Connor in the Fair Field and great chewing in them if you had the teeth for it, which I had always. Signs by, I liked my grandfather's house and seldom passed the door without calling to see him.

My father's father lived a few streets away from us and sometimes I dropped in on him to see if there were a few pennies stirring. A tailor he was and he had a big beard and two wives, and men with beards and two voyages into marriage were rare enough in the town in those days anyway. He was a fine figure of a man, over six feet and straight as a candle, and shoulders broad to flatten the mountain. Patsy Hoare told me that he once saw him jumping the spiked railway-gate beside the RIC barracks with his boots on and I didn't see any wonder in that. After all, he was my grandfather, wasn't he.

Unlike my small grandfather, he did not encourage visits from talkative boys. He had his work to do, and, while my mother's father had only a handful of grandchildren to cope with, he had no less than eighteen. He never threw me out or anything, he just stitched away silently and silence is a weapon few boys, or men for that matter, can fight against for long. I used to go out to the backyard and play with the flush lavatory. The likes of it was a novelty to me and I could never understand why it didn't flow over, and drown the street. I wasted enough water trying to find out anyway but rain was plentiful and no one died from thirst on account of my antics.

Not very big the town was but Small Daddy, as we called him, rarely met Big Grandfather. One was a tradesman (and, needless to add, a good one) and the other after a life of fishing for mackerel and tilling the soil now ambled at his ease up to Primrose Wood every other day for a load of branches to keep the fireplace contented. On Sunday Big Grandfather laid down the needle, grabbed a stick, whistled to his dog and went up Carhan river hunting water-rats. Small Daddy usually remained indoors on that day, smoking his pipe and belting away in Irish to my Granny. After all, it was a day of rest and in Small Daddy's eyes occupations like going to football matches and roaming the country with dogs were anything but restful.

Small Daddy came from Ballinskelligs and Irish was his first language, as it was my grandmother's. They rarely spoke English when they were in the house although they had the full of a dictionary of it when they liked. I never ceased to wonder at the easy way Irish flowed from them, especially when I had been lambasted in school a few hours before for not knowing the genitive case of 'Bróg.' English only my father had and that was the language in our house.

'Hard for him to have the Irish,' Small Daddy remarked, 'and his father a foreigner from Caragh Bridge.'

Small Daddy always conveniently forgot that Big Grandfather had come to live in the town years before himself.

I was reared a strong Republican and I found it hard to forgive Small Daddy his love of Royalty. In his tobacco-pouch he kept a shining half-penny with the head of Queen Victoria on it. Every time he took out the square of plug for cutting he used place the half-penny carefully on the table in case he lost it. For years I watched the ritual and then I asked him why he always carried Victoria's half-penny in his pouch.

'The copper in it gives a grand taste to the tobacco,' he told me.

There have been worse reasons than that for treasuring the head of a queen.

Small Daddy had three great cronies, Mickey Devane, Paddy the Watch and Mike Burke down the Lane. Mike lived alone and they all met in his house every second night where they could talk the black hats off each other without any interrupting women to annoy them. One dark October night Joe Whelan, myself, and a couple of other young scoundrels paid the Lane a visit. We crouched outside the window listening and a waste of good hearing it was for the Irish was pouring out of them like buttermilk from a jug, and we couldn't fathom a tittle of it.

We tied a length of rope to the latch and held on while Joe Whelan with his big hobnails began to kick the door down.

There was a silence inside that you could shave with Finn Mac Cool's razor.

'Come out and fight, Burke, if you're a man,' Joe roared.

'Come on out, Sigerson, and I'll do for you! Rise out of it, you band of cowards!'

And all the time the poor old door shivering under a volley of kicks to lame an elephant.

The rest of us were laughing so fiercely we could hardly stand up. Scoundrels we were and deserving to be denied Christian burial, and that could happen yet for we are all very much alive still. But, sweet stars of Spain, it was a delicious moment and remembered for ever.

Mike was tugging at the door from the inside now and using strong English in case we'd misunderstand him, and Joe gave him back vowel for consonant, and the door plenty of the boot, and calling them all out to their destruction.

We were too happy laughing to see the window over our heads opening slowly and Small Daddy there with a bucket which he silently tilted. Joe got most of it, and rightly so, and I came off the best myself for I was at the end of the rope. And it wasn't spring water was in that bucket either.

Going to the wood for branches with Small Daddy was an adventure I loved. Up the Road of the Streams we went, past Michael Griffin's well, across the shoulder of Pat Driscoll's hill, and down into Primrose Wood. A bag of questions I had for him about everything I saw and heard, bird, flower, bush, beetle or forest giant. He gave me the names of them all and told me the story of how everything got its name the first day. Afterwards I discovered that he had the wrong names for the most of them, but what matter when the stories were good to entertain! Imagination is everything in a world going fast to the devil with realism.

Around Hallowe'en he commenced tossing off the ghost stories. He was good to set the stage for he never bothered to tell one in the summer when the bright nights whipped the magic out of it. A dark night he wanted and the wick of the oil-lamp down low, and if there was a bit of a banshee wind olagowning down the chimney so much the better. A library of stories he had, one weirder than the other, and in them cloven-footed men, headless horses, talking conger-eels and unlicensed dogs with eyes like motor-bulbs followed one after the other as plentiful as the June swallows on the river. Compared with Small Daddy, Kitty the Hare was only in the infant-class in the Ghosttown University.

No wonder I saw more ghosts by Eugie Neill's black shed on my way home than you'd meet at midnight in Glasnevin graveyard after a hurricane. To tell the naked truth I still see the devils on the rare occasions I pass there and the darkness in it.

When I was eleven years old Small Daddy died and the candle at which I warmed my hands was quenched for ever.

Still, the richest boy in the town I was to have a grandfather the likes of him.

4. The Trapper

When Cobbler Carthy's pipe was smoked to ashes, he arose and flicked his eyes over the birds swinging from the rafters in our house, the two goldfinches by the back door and the red-breasted linnet beside the dresser.

'Which is the best, Tom?' he asked my father. My father pointed at the nearest goldfinch.

'Dick there is the champion. The best bird I have handled. He'd crack the rafters for you. I wouldn't swap that fellow for a fifty acre farm.'

'He must be good so,' agreed the cobbler. He took the cover from his pipe and knocked the ashes carefully into the fire as he saw my mother's eye trained on him.

'I suppose,' he continued, 'you've noticed the wife's niece staying with us for the past week?'

'I have,' said my father. 'A fine healthy girl she is God bless her.'

'Well,' said the cobbler, coming to the point at last, 'the Glenbay Trapper sent a challenge by her. He'll meet you on Sunday week, weather permitting, in Reardon's field by the river. The first man to trap a goldfinch wins and the winner gets his opponent's call-bird for a prize. Are you agreeable?'

My father, who was the best bird trapper in our parish, nodded. 'I'm agreeable. I haven't any bird-lime at the moment, but I can make some tomorrow. Sunday week, you said? Tell the Glenbay Trapper I'll be there.'

The cobbler moved towards the half-door.

''Twill be a good contest and this parish will have a stocking of money on you. The girl is going home this evening and I'll send your message by her. Good luck now, whatever.'

On the day of the contest, I was the proudest lad since Lucifer and I left the house with Dick, the call bird, swinging by my side, and my father on my left hand with his head held high as befitting a champion on his way to up-hold the honour of his parish. At the bottom of the Rocky Road the bird-men, fully a score of them, were waiting on us. We all marched two by two like Dooley's army to the river.

When we arrived we found the Glenbay Trapper and his supporters sprawled on the grass by the river's edge. He rose to his feet and shook hands with my father. He nodded at Dick in his green cage.

'That's a good finch you have, Tom,' he told my father.

'Mhuise,' deprecated my father, 'he's only middling.'

As he had a Glenbay wife and, in consequence, a leg in each parish, Cobbler Carty was elected judge. He called the contestants to him and explained the rules.

He tossed a penny for choice of position in the field and my father won. As we walked away from the men the cobbler shouted, 'Lay your bets now, lads,' and we could hear the snapping of catches as the careful country purses opened and shut. Reardon's field, which grew most of the parish's crop of thistles, was a favourite feeding-ground of the goldfinches.

My father who had spent many hours bird-watching from the bushes that rimmed it, walked straight to the eastern corner and stood the cage among the purple thistles. Then he spat on his fingers and limed the sprig he had brought with him. We went back to the bushes and waited.

It was agony hiding there in the leaves, listening to the airy chatter of the men and the placid drone of the river, and peering about the sky for the expected birds. I looked at my father. He was quite silent, his face white and tense as he stared steadfastly at the east.

A nerve in his neck throbbed against the skin as though there were a little spring bubbling somewhere in his throat.

His long thin fingers fidgeted like aspen leaves. It was the first time I saw him really nervous.

Below us the Glenbay Trapper suddenly whistled and pointed to the south-east. We looked and saw the charm of goldfinches high in the sky and as they came nearer we could hear the tinkle of their twittering like silver coins tossed among stones. Bigger and louder they grew until they were flying above the field.

'They won't land,' said someone in a fierce whisper. 'Bad luck to them, they suspect something.'

Then Dick, our call-bird, began to sing. Music gushed from his small pulsing throat, louder and louder until the field and sky throbbed with it. Bright-eyed I listened and fancied I could see the notes surging upwards in a silver wave to drench the goldfinches flying overhead.

'God!' cried the cobbler excitedly, 'that's what I call a song bird. Whist! Whist! He's bringing them down.'

And he was. Suddenly the charm stopped dead and swished to earth like a fistful of flung gravel. They crowded the thistles about Dick's cage, peering at him with their crimson heads cocked sideways and fluttering their dainty yellow wings.

Breathlessly we watched them, every man-jack of us stiff as stone statues behind the screen of bushes. Then a voice husky with excitement began to shout, 'There's a finch on Tom Duggan's sprig. Quick, Tom, quick.'

But my father had already burst through the bushes and was tearing across the field, his big boots shaking the earth. The charm rose in a coloured cloud at his coming and flew off twittering to the west.

My father flung himself on his knees beside the trapped bird and we could see his shoulders moving as he took it from the sprig.

And then, instead of running back to us, he remained kneeling there, his body petrified, his head bowed to the ground. The men of our parish shifted their feet angrily as they began to shout at him. 'What's wrong with you, man?

Wake up, Tom, and don't be falling asleep on the job. Will you hurry on to hell out of there!'

The cobbler turned and glared at them. 'Fair play for the Glenbay Trapper,' he roared. 'The contest isn't over yet.'

Puzzled I stared at the bent stiff figure of my father and then I heard the twittering in the sky and I looked up. A solitary goldfinch, a straggler from the charm, was dipping towards the field. The Glenbay bird burst into song and he dived to greet him. He circled the cage twice and perched on the limed sprig. I closed my eyes tight as I saw the Glenbay Trapper charging across the field. When I opened them he was putting the trapped bird into the cobbler's hand and the shouting of the delighted Glenbay men was cracking the sky. I turned away from them and ran like mad to my father, the tears streaming down my face.

'Faad,' I cried, 'Oh! Fadd, what happened you? Are you sick or what?' He opened his fist and showed me a goldfinch lying limp in his palm.

'I killed him,' he said sadly. 'God forgive me, I killed the little fellow taking him off the sprig.'

I groped around for words to say something comforting to him but I couldn't find any. The Glenbay trapper came swaggering across to us and my father gave him our call-bird. 'You were unlucky to lose, Tom,' he told my father.

He went back to his friends and they marched down the road to their own parish, cheering loudly. I stood beside my father among the purple thistles and we looked after them until the cheering died away.

5. Master Melody

John Melody, retired schoolmaster, closed the door of his lodging-house in Main Street, Ballytwig, behind him and walked briskly towards the eastern end of the village. He was in his usual good humour and he hummed as he walked. The catchy air of a song, about one leaving Donegal he had just heard on the wireless, nested in his brain and refused to be evicted, and he would go on humming it until some other ditty took its place. He was a small, rotund, red-cheeked man, cheery-looking like a Christmas cracker; his face always shaved as clean as a whistle.

The street was bare except for a black-and-tan beagle, and a brown horse anchored to the electric-light pole outside Canty's pub. When he came by the animal he lifted his hat courteously and said: 'Good evening, Horse'. The horse jingled his head harness as though in reply and the Master chuckled. He liked animals and, with the exception of Bill Carroll's bull, which once made him swim the river with his clothes on, they liked him.

He always saluted horses, no matter how important the person in his company at the time. When he landed in Ballytwig forty odd years ago the villagers had stared in amazement at this idiosyncrasy of his and wondered if he was really a schoolmaster. They expected their teachers to have dignity, which meant wearing a stern, unsmiling face and not lifting your hat to a horse. The Master ignored the pained and puzzled expressions, and beamed upon the good citizens like a rich American uncle. Then they found him shaping successful scholars from the rude clay that was their sons, and they decided that he was a genius, and as such entitled to be something out of the ordinary in what he said or did.

There was the evening he walked from the school with the Inspector who had come to sit in judgement upon him. Mike Donnelly's horse stood under a rail of turf outside the Emporium. He saw the Master coming and threw up his head in greeting. The Master lifted his hat and said: 'Good evening, Tom'. The Inspector blinked and looked hard at him. He was a grim man with the weight of the world, the stars, and the planets on his narrow shoulders, and when they'd come to button the coffin about him nobody would mourn his passing and only the inscription over his grave would remember him until the moss covered it.

'Do you usually salute horses in public, Melody?' he had asked, the thin lips making a ruler of his mouth.

'Only when they salute me,' the Master answered gravely. 'Some of them can be quite snobbish, you know. Just like humans.'

The horse neighed behind them.

'Old Tom is vexed with me. I usually have a square of sugar for him. You don't happen to have a lump in your pocket, Inspector?'

'Certainly not,' snapped the Inspector.

He turned the corner to his hotel, and the Master went in his own door chuckling merrily. He got out his diary and wrote the events of the day.

'Inspector Dancy called. A sour ill-humoured body. He wouldn't talk to a pig. What does he get from life?'

In the hotel the Inspector penned his report to the Department.

'Mister Melody has his pupils in excellent shape, but the man himself strikes me as being mental. He completely lacks dignity and holds conversations with horses on the village streets.'

The Master's evening walk always took him past the old school, down Pat Dannigh's Height and on to the Three Eye Bridge where he usually stopped to light up his pipe and study the life that flowed over and under the grey humpy arches. The brown trout splashing in the pools, and the small eels wriggling across the stones, swallows stunting under the tent of the sky, brown rabbits slipping through the briars, had always given him a measure of comfort, and now that he was alone and lonely he turned to them for consolation. He had never married, his school was shuttered and deserted, his pupils had grown, scattered and married, and were sending their sons to the Brothers. His school among the hazels now served as a windbreak for cattle when the storms blew in from the sea.

As he drew near the school he heard Dick Sullivan's voice raised in a come-all-ye behind the screen of hazel bushes, and the rattle of a hammer upon slates. He slipped through the broken gate and looked up. Dick was straddling the roof, stripping the slates and letting them slide down to the grass. The Master felt himself grow cold as he watched.

'Richard!' he called out after a while. Sullivan stopped working and waved to him.

'Hello, Master,' he greeted him.

'What are you doing to our old school, Richard?'

'I'm taking it home with me, Master. I bought the stones to build a cowhouse. 'Twill remind me of old times every time I milk the cows in it. I hope the cows will learn easier than I did anyway. Wisha, do you remember, Master, the composition I did for the Inspector?'

The Master remembered, smiling as he did so, in spite of the pain in his mind. Dancy had ordered the pupils to write an essay on a walk in the country, to test their powers of observation. Afterwards he read some of them to the school as examples of clear writing and clearer observation. Before he read Dick's, which he kept like good wine for the last, he described it as a classic which should not on any account be plagiarised. It was short and sweet and no nonsense.

'A Walk in the Country. I went for a walk yesterday evening around by Mulvey's Mill. I saw nobody and nobody saw me. Richard Sullivan.'

The Master continued towards the river, his brain numbed by the sacrilege of his school's destruction. To him it was not an inanimate thing with a coat of whitewash and a helmet of slate. It was a boy in a gansey, who threw away his shoes when May pinned the stars to the hawthorn, and ran over the long butter-cupped grass among the hazel trees. It had a voice that chanted the death of Master Tommy Rook, or King Bruce and the Spider, or shrilled into battle with Kelly of Killane when Mrs Casey came once a week for the music-hour. It had an untidy thatch of hair and a forehead that worried itself into corrugated-iron wrinkles over the speed of trains per hour and the profit or loss on shiploads of tea from Ceylon. It was half a century of boys. His boys.

The following evening on his way to the river he slipped through the broken gate again. The roof was stripped and the rafters were naked and lean in the cold air. Dick Sullivan stood smoking and talking to Timmy the Boots from Donegan's Hotel. Timmy had been one of his favourite pupils at school and his devoted ally afterwards. No Inspector could steal a march on him with Timmy meeting the trains and ready to hop on his bicycle and burn up the half-mile to the school while you'd be winking.

'There's a strange man with a small brown case after coming on the 11 o'clock, Master. He's not a commercial so, maybe, he's from the Department.'

'Thank you, Timmy. Now that we are forewarned you can rest assured the Department will have sufficient reason to think highly of scholarship in Ballytwig.'

Only once did an Inspector catch him napping, but that wasn't Timmy's fault. It was the time the heat wave flattened Ballytwig which was so used to rain that it nearly died of thirst and too much sunshine after a week of it. The boys turned listlessly in their desks and wiped the perspiration from their freckles. The Master went to open the window wider and saw the sandbanks one hundred yards away, brown and wet and beautiful, possessed by gulls and oyster-catchers. He turned to the pupils and announced with mock gravity:

'I am now going to the sandbanks for a swim. You can have the choice of coming with me or staying in your desks.'

They were already in the sea when he arrived, the skilful twisting and turning like otters, the beginners splashing and shouting in the shallows. He slipped into his bathing costume and the sand squeezed itself soft and hot between his toes.

'Is the water warm, boys?' he called out.

'You could hatch a goose's egg in it, Master,' declared Dick Sullivan who made up in the spoken word all he lacked in the written.

After his swim he sat in the sun, watching them enjoying themselves as though they had been locked away in some dark cave for twelve months. A few years and they would nearly all be scattered, he thought, in London or Boston or Melbourne, pining for the sea on the brown sand, and the majesty of the mountains. They would ——

'Master!'

Dick was beside him whispering urgently.

'Yes, Richard?'

'There's a strange man after leaving the school and he's coming this way. Maybe he's an Inspector. He has the brown bag anyway.'

The Master looked over his shoulder and saw the stranger crossing the fields. He pursed his lips and sighed.

'Richard, I fear we are undone. Swim away, my boy, and enjoy yourselves while I have a word with him.'

The stranger towered over the Master like a light-house. He had blue eyes that twinkled and the mouth under the grey moustache was humorous. He was Inspector O'Toole, he said, and Dancy was in hospital suffering from the Bubonic plague or some such ailment, and he was doing the Dancy rounds. The devil is as droll as myself, thought the Master, and he began to complain of the heat wave and the boys wilting like cut flowers in their desks, so he thought it wiser to freshen them up a bit before one of them died on his hands.

'You took a leaf from the copy-book of Ancient Greece,' smiled the Inspector.

'Yes, Inspector, I believe the Greeks have a word for it,' said the Master.

'The Department has one, too, Mister Melody, but we won't give them the chance to use it. I think I'll join you in a swim. I have a costume in my case.'

Afterwards the Inspector gathered the boys about him and flung questions at them while the Master stood aside, silently praying that the angel of inspiration would settle his wings over them for that day at least. And, indeed, the water that entered their ears must have cleansed their brains, for they spoke out as though the answers were written on the sand in front of them.

That evening while Mrs Sweeney was making his tea, the Master took out his diary.

'On very rare occasions,' he wrote, 'a man is born into this world and all the bells of heaven ring out loud and clear to announce his birth. Such a man is Inspector O'Toole.'

The Inspector wrote his report in his motor-car, lifting his head now and again to watch the sun setting behind the western islands.

'..... In a mad, bad world it is refreshing to meet a man of Mr Melody's splendid sanity. His pupils are the most intelligent I have met in my travels. I was struck also by their cleanliness, and I must be pardoned for thinking that he may have heard of my coming and had them all washed especially for me.'

Every evening the Master walked out the road and watched the school shrinking like a six-penny shirt. The spring was going from his step now and he was so busy with his thoughts that he failed to return the salutations from the people he met on the way. The Master is failing, they told each other, and you'd swear a few weeks ago that he'd live to be as old as a bush in a fairy fort.

He spent the day before Christmas Eve in bed, and he

wouldn't have done it if Mrs Sweeney hadn't bullied him into resting. He had lodged under her roof so long now she became alarmed at the thought of losing him. And these men who were never a day sick in their lives were always the quickest to go in the heel of the hunt. Never having known illness they hadn't the wits to fight it when it came.

On Christmas Eve he heard the door close behind Mrs Sweeney as she went to meet her two daughters, with civil service jobs in Dublin, who were arriving on the six o'clock train. He got out of bed and dressed himself, and went into the street. The shops were still wide awake and brisk with selling, and a mournful ballad ribboned out of a public house to make the night lonesome.

He went out the road slowly, leaning on his stick, until he came to the broken gate. He groped in and looked for his school. There was nothing at all left of it now except the moonlit black squares that next spring's grass would wipe off the slate for good.

A great tiredness enveloped him and he sat down on a big stone inside the gate. The candles were burning in the mountainy windows across the estuary and, as he watched them, they began to advance and retire like dancers. And then, suddenly, they were quenched.

Dick Sullivan with his horse and cart came singing out of the village. He passed by the gate where the Master was huddled. He saw nobody. And nobody saw him.

6. Daddo's Shilling

Daddo was my grandfather and Nan was my grandmother and they lived in a small house wedged in the middle of the forty other small houses of Turret Street. I lodged with them because my parents also had a little house and ten children to take the bare look off it. When my mother persuaded Nan to take one of us to her house the old lady lined us all up on the kitchen floor and scrutinised us as though we had measles or small-pox or something.

'Wasn't God good and to send me only the one daughter,' she said turning us around to the light to see the colour of our eyes.

Nan was a great believer in the virtues of a blue eye and we must have been a sore disappointment to her, for the ten of us had two brown eyes each and if we had a third eye that would be brown too I suppose.

'I'll take Sonny,' she decided in the end. 'He has the look of my own poor father about him.' I wasn't too pleased at the compliment, for her own poor father had been no great shakes. When he had a pint of poteen in him he always marched off with a pike to attack the police-barracks, but he always sobered up before he reached it. Indeed, the old man's forays were a sore trial to me at school where the fellows that didn't like me remembered the phrase 'When Tadg More captures the police-barracks,' which was another way of saying never. If you weren't a warrior in our valley there was scant respect for you and if you were the descendant of a half-warrior like Tadg Mor you were blamed often enough for the foibles of your ancestors.

Daddo had so many ghost stories he must have been a ghost himself one time. I sat wide-eyed beside the fire listening to the exploits of the black dogs, headless men, women with two heads to make up for the men, death-coaches and banshees until in the end I was afraid to go to the well for water after dark.

'You'll frighten the foolish brown eyes out of the fledgling's head,' Nan warned him in Irish.

They always spoke Irish when they didn't want me to understand and that was the rock they perished on for the Master had walloped plenty of it into my skull from an early age. And, besides, the brand of English we favoured in the valley was half-Irish.

Every Friday night Daddo and Nan had a row over a shilling and that was the only kind of stinging-match that ever took place between them while I was living in the house.

On Fridays after dinner Daddo clapped the black wide-awake hat on his head, lit his pipe, grabbed his blackthorn stick and stumped off to the post office for his pension.

'Twould be facing bedtime before he used show up and a smell of porter from him that would kick down a goal-post. Nan would shoot out her hand before he had time to say, 'God bless all here'.

'I suppose the shilling is missing again this time, you little hedgehog,' she'd shrill.

''Tisn't then, I hope,' by Daddo. 'I spent a white florin only on porter and I should have the other eight shillings safe in the cashbox for you, my bright love.'

But though he searched himself hard and Nan searched him harder still, no more than seven shillings was ever found.

He went up to bed then to snore like a sea-lion and Nan used turn to me.

'He's a bigger liar than Cromwell. Kneel down boyeen bawn, and we'll offer up the Rosary for him for he'll never get to Heaven on his own.'

And the following morning Daddo always went down to the pubs on the Main Street to squander the mysterious shilling on what he called his 'cure'.

In the end the missing shilling played so much on Nan's nerves that she could hardly sleep worrying over it. It was beginning to annoy me, too, for I prided myself on my cleverness as a searcher, but Daddo was too cute for the pair of us.

One fine Friday evening Nan sent me in search of Daddo with instructions to wheedle the hiding-place out of him and let her know. I found Daddo in Casey's Snug at bay before a pack of foaming pints of porter, and telling his stories to a laughing ring of admirers, who were decent enough not to expect entertainment for nothing. He came out of the snug when he saw me.

'What ails her now, garsoon?' he asked.

'She told me to find out where you hide the shilling, Daddo, and let her know,' I told him.

'Did she, faith?' said Daddo with a wink that nearly squeezed porter out of his eyelids.

'She did, Daddo,' I assured him. 'But even if you did tell me I wouldn't make her wise.'

'You're a good garsoon,' Daddo praised me: 'Here's a red penny for you now and run home and tell Nan I'll show her the hiding-place when Tadg Mor captures the police-barrack.'

Into the snug with him again as though he was being reared in it.

When he was in bed that night we searched his hat, clothes and boots but there was no trace of the shilling.

'I know him like the cat knows boiling milk,' said Nan, 'and he has that shilling on him somewhere.'

But in spite of her, Daddo was out of the house at ten o'clock the following morning and belting off for Main Street for a couple of hairs of the black dog.

Three years later Nan died. Daddo and myself were with her after the priest had gone when she whispered to him for the last time.

'Wisha, where used you hide the shilling on me, Daddo?' she asked.

Daddo pulled out his pipe and removed the cover from it. He took her hand and a shilling fell from the bowl of the pipe into her palm. She closed her fingers over it and smiled up at him. Daddo wouldn't be too cute for her any more now.

7. The Rebel

He was such a small, wizened, bright-eyed man, the dead spit of the imagined leprechaun, that if you came across him in a lonely place and didn't know who he was you'd have him by the throat in a wink to throttle the pot of gold out of him. Not that poor Jureen Madden had any of the yellow stuff hidden away.

He was a kind, gentle fellow of sixty-five, unmarried, and he kept the house together for his brother, Dan, who was employed by the county council to keep the roads fit for the tourists to drive on. Dan was a huge man, a year older than Jureen, dour and silent, who spoke only on Saturday nights when his Adam's apple floated on the back tide of half-a-dozen pints.

Dan blamed Jureen for the emptiness of his life with no wife or children to put an edge to it. When their mother was dying she had called Dan to hear her last message.

'He's the delicate one, Dan, and if you don't look after him he'll be tied to the skilly-pot in the county home. If you ever throw him out in the cold I'll hop back from the grave to you.'

Dan fully believed she could come back if she had a mind to, and he kept Jureen close to the hob except when he went down town for the grub to feed the two of them. He had asked three women to marry him but they refused unless Jureen was tossed out the half-door, and Dan's fear of a dead mother outweighed his desire for a live wife. He stopped courting after the third refusal and took to the porter.

When he came home from the pub on Saturday nights and saw Jureen smoking his pipe beside the fire the anger nearly choked him.

'Puffing away you are as though they willed you the tobacco factory! Where would you be only for me? In the county home! That's where you'd have your abode, you ciaroge!'

'Will I wet a scald of tay for you, Dan?'

'You'll wet nothing, you changeling!'

To bed with him then to snore and hold his tongue until the next Saturday night when the porter boiled in him again. Every month the pay-cheque came from the county council and when Dan signed it he handed it to Jureen who cashed it with Tom Driscoll, the grocer, and paid him any money owing. The balance he tied carefully in his handkerchief and gave to Dan that evening when he strode in, shovel on shoulder, from the roads.

For forty years since their mother died Jureen had followed the ritual of the cheque-cashing without stepping an inch out of line. And then in September of the forty-first year he hit against Boston Sullivan as he was coming out of Driscoll's shop with the month's money in his fist. Boston home from America on a holiday, embraced him, dragged him in to Hogan's pub and threw a large whiskey into him. The whiskey marched around inside Jureen's stomach like a piper's band and his lost manhood came back to him at a gallop. He opened the knotted handkerchief and insisted on Boston having another glass. They drank and then the pub began to sprout hands that came to welcome Boston home and remained to down the whiskies that himself and Jureen paid for, Boston in Uncle Sam's money and Jureen in Brother Dan's. When Jureen's capital was reduced to seven shillings he stumbled into the street and stood there swaying. There was a mist bothering his eyes and now and then it lifted and he could see Dan's outraged eyes glaring at him. Fear nibbled under the roof of his skull and he decided to run away. He staggered to the railway station and peered in the ticket-hole. 'How much is the ticket to Ballysally?' he asked the clerk.

'Six and tenpence,' he was told.

'Throw one out to me so,' said Jureen.

When he arrived at the county home the nurse took him to the recreation room and put him under the wing of another guest, Charlie Donoghue. There were men playing cards or draughts or reading quietly and when Charlie told them who Jureen was they all smiled and bid him welcome. Then Charlie brought out his fiddle and tossed off a few hornpipes to lift the heart in him.

'Have you any old stave of a song in you?' Charlie asked him.

'I got a bag of them from my father only I had no occasion to sing them these years,' Jureen told him.

'Yerra, you might as well sing grief as cry it,' said Charlie. 'Give tongue now and I'll be with you on the fiddle.'

Jureen sang. He had a pleasant voice and the song was so old nobody had ever heard it before. When he was finished they all clapped and Charlie praised him highly because 'he had a sweet crying voice that was getting very rare now the people were learning to speak the English.'

He dug out a half a dozen other old ballads about moonlighters and poteen-making, and daughters of the gentry who ran away with handsome ploughmen to America. By bedtime he was the most popular man in the home and for the first time in his life his mouth was full of happiness. One man told him he was Ireland's best and Charlie said he was the greatest discovery since tobacco. Jureen began to think that maybe he was dead after all and had found his way into heaven.

''Tis like a hotel, man,' he told Charlie, the following day when they went to examine the town.

Then the local schoolmaster who collected songs and folklore and who was decent with his whiskey heard about him and called with pen and paper to record Jureen's store for posterity.

'If you ran away when you were fourteen there's no knowing where you'd be,' Charlie praised.

A month after leaving Dan the nurse came into the room as he was smoking and listening contentedly to Charlie twisting a hornpipe off the fiddle.

'Jureen,' she told him, 'your brother Dan wants you to come back. He's on the phone outside now and wishes to speak to you.'

Charlie stopped playing and looked at him. The card-players straightened and turned their heads to him. Jureen took the pipe from his mouth and blew out a puff of smoke.

'Tell him Nurse,' he said, 'tell him I'm not at home.'

8. The Master's Girl

From where Jamsie Shea sat under the heavy seine-boat oar he could see the child's handful of lights that was Portmaura village winking in the lap of the mountain. He stared at them and pinned down the windows that sprouted them. The dim light to the west would be Miser Mick's house. He never cracked a match to anything dearer than a half-penny candle and it was seldom enough he did that same. 'Every copper a prisoner,' the village wag said his motto was.

The paraffin-fed light next door was the Widow MacCarthy's, a snug woman with a slate house and a bold-eyed daughter, Nonie, who had big hands and a laugh like a man. And the very bright light to the extreme west was Master Connolly's. He sighed and began to think of the master's daughter, Una.

Seán a'Dost who shared the heavy oar with him elbowed his ribs and he looked up to find his father shouting at him from the tiller. 'If 'tis sleep you want, boy, I'll make a bed for you,' he scoffed in Gaelic. The other fishermen, all of them rearing families, began to pelt him with fistfuls of their coarse heavy humour. He smiled and shrugged his shoulders until they tired of it and general conversation tilted through the boat again.

He was not in the mood to talk and he was glad to be partner to Seán at the rowing. Seán a'Dost, John of the Silences, always had a pipe clenched between his teeth and rarely spoke. The humorists cracked that when Seán went to confession he wrote down his sins in a copy-book for the priest. Now that Jamsie wanted to remember Una, it was heaven itself to be rowing with a man like Silent John.

His eyes sought out the quivering dandelion of light again. She would be busy now, he supposed, packing her things into the two big brown cases he saw in the house when he called to say goodbye to her. The master would be fussing over her, an untidy old hen of a man, scattering threadbare proverbs like feathers everywhere: A stitch in time saves nine; You can't make a silk purse out of a sow's ear. All that glistens is not gold. A great man for proverbs was the master, in school and out of it.

They had gone to the same school, he and Una, where Master Connolly taught the boys, and Miss Donnelly, as the master declared in his cups, made an effort to make genteel ladies out of the girls. Miss Donnelly was fat, wore spectacles, chewed peppermints and had a strong right arm as some of the boys discovered when she caught them peeping through the hole in the partition that separated the classes.

Master Connolly like Aaron believed in his Rod, and had a collection of picturesque phrases that had grown dog-eared from use. 'He has a head like Pontius Pilate's horse,' he used say as he pilloried some youthful offender, or 'Look at the cut of him! The rats must have been sucking his hair all night,' or 'There's a smell of the devil in this room. I tell ye I'll root it out.'

Looking back at it all now from the comparative safety of a seine-boat, it was amusing — though at the time it put the fear of God into one's heart.

His way ran past Una's house and they often went home together after school. He grew older, became girl-conscious, and began to avoid her, dallying about the school in the evening until she had turned the bend in the road. She lay in ambush for him and challenged him about his change of face towards her. He led her to the quay wall and showed it to her. 'J.S. courting U.C.' in crude tarred letters six inches high. She laughed and tossed back her yellow hair. 'Why don't you rub it out?' she asked. But he didn't want to rub it out. He wanted it to stay there for ever, to blaze out like a rainbow until the whole world would see and admire it, now he knew she didn't mind.

It was there yet, wind and weather had been kind to it, a bit pale and faded but still readable. 'J.S. courting U.C.'

Master Connolly became too old to use the rod effectively though he still had a viper in his tongue. Jamsie's father, granite-hard realist that he was, took him from school to till the patch of land, that was so small a hen couldn't mark time on it, and to sit under an oar in the seine-boat. Una, dressed like a princess, went off to college, her golden hair glowing under a round hat, and for him, the glen was a graveyard while she was away.

When she arrived home for the Christmas holidays he called to see her. She had grown up, had changed, her eyes were focused on far distances as she spoke to him. He realised she was not for him, that the tarred inscription on the quay wall could well be obliterated now. He still visited the master's house.

His father looked at him darkly, and mouthed a warning. 'She's no fisherman's wife, lad, or no farmer's wife either. Leave her after you, son. The world is wide.' He answered nothing, but kept on visiting. The world was wide, very wide, and she was going out into it. He had to stay behind, fiddling with the patch of earth by day, hauling the nets by night....

An elbow poked his ribs again and he turned to see Silent John nodding towards the tiller where his father stood, spear-straight, peering intently into the distance. He shifted in his seat and looked in the same direction. Away near the horizon a six-pence of light glowed on the face of the sea. It moved towards them swiftly, growing bigger as it came, the little phosphorescent flames dancing on the waters until it appeared as if the sea itself was on fire. Mackerel.

In the stern his father began to beat the air with his fist. 'O thuaidh! O thuaidh! Mackerel from the north! Nets out, nets out!' he shouted.

The men dropped their nets and hauled until the boat was loaded to the gunwale with fish. The mackerel wriggled and slithered across each other, their tails slapping impotently, their bodies burning like rainbows. There was so much light in the boat it seemed as though they had netted half the stars in heaven. Then they folded their nets and went over the sea to home.

It was nearing the dawn when he walked the road to Master Connolly's house. He went to the door and listened. Nothing stirred there. He fastened a string of mackerel to the latch and went out on the road again. His father was there waiting for him. He nodded towards the house.

''Twill be a long time again before the master's daughter eats a fresh mackerel,' he said.

''Twill,' Jamsie agreed.

'She's going to some queer foreign place I believe.'

'She's going to Africa.'

'To be a nun!'

'Yes.'

'I never thought she had the makings of a nun in her,' said his father. He did not answer. They walked in silence to their own house. Outside the door they stopped and listened. Somewhere in the hills a cart was rattling across the stones.

'That'll be a few Kilbreena boys going to London,' said his father.

'The Donoghues are going,' said Jamsie.

'What would they be doing in London away from the sea?' asked his father. Jamsie did not reply. It was bright now in the east and at the little railway station six miles away an engine puffing petulantly was shunting. He watched it thoughtfully for a few minutes.

'Did Curran, the fish-buyer, give you any money for me this evening?' asked his father.

'He gave me £5, I have it here with me.'

'Hold on to it so. You'll be needing a new suit.'

'I have a new suit already,' he said.

'You'll need another — a marriage suit,' said his father. 'Mickey the Matchmaker was talking to me today. The Widow MacCarthy wants you for her daughter, Nonie. She has a fortune of £300. 'Twill buy the bit of land beside this place for ye. You'll marry her this day month.'

'Whatever you say,' replied Jamsie.

His father moved into the house and left him alone. He looked downwards. Connolly's chimney wore a blue plume of smoke and he watched it waver and break in the light wind. At the station the engine shunted up and down like a kitten playing with its tail. He thrust his hand in his pocket and felt the pound notes crisping under his fingers.

He turned, flung his oilskins from him, and got his bike out of the shed. He wheeled it down the boreen to the main road and mounted it. The main road ran downhill all the way to the station .....

9. The Go-Getter

Only one chestnut grew in the glen and the roots of it were anchored in the Old Road, between Ulick Donoghue's house and the mountain. My father told me one morning that it was in blossom and to run up and see it.

I ran down the street, climbed the gate of the big meadow and took the short cut to the tree. Rain had fallen during the night and the wet grass rubbed white patches into my shoes. The larks held a shining umbrella of song over my head as I ran.

The hills had clean faces with every tooth of rock scrubbed until it shone like a shilling. There was so much blue in the sky it seemed as though the sky had fallen.

What is there more beautiful than a chestnut tree in blossom? I skipped up the boreen between the houses and suddenly I was beside it and all the loveliness of it was pouring over me in a white, shining wave.

Ten feet from the earth the branches began and from there to the high tip-top of it, blossom piled on blossom until you could hardly see the green leaves for the pink whiteness. Like the high altar in the chapel it was when it is Benediction-time and a thousand candles tremble with their golden petals of flame, and the incense floats up from the swinging thurible and the organ makes mighty sea-noises as the priest chants the Latin.

I stood there watching the tree and some strange delicacy of mind sent the tears flooding into my eyes.

'What are you crying about?'

I shook the water from my eyes and saw Ulick in front of me.

'A midge flew into my eye,' I said quickly.

'You're lucky it was only a midge. A bumble bee struck against mine yesterday and he nearly blinded me for life. Look.'

Dark brown eyes he had, rich with strong sight, and in the white of one a mesh of red threads twisting and angry.

''Twill be all right next week though; Shawn Oge told me it would and isn't he half a doctor. He cures all the sick cows and horses for the farmers.'

He moved over to the tree, put his hand on it and swung around it the way a carefree child circles a lamp-post in the street.

'This is my tree,' he said. 'Jacky Dee next door claimed it as his but I fought him for it.'

'Did you win, Ulick?'

'I beat him and his mother chased me with a brush.'

He left the tree and came to me.

'Come on, we'll go up Carhan and look for birds' nests,' he said.

I whipped off my shoes and the grey stockings with the necklace of twinkling red diamonds about the tops of them, and hid them in the branches of Ulick's tree. Then we ran along the path behind the houses and came to Mickey Art's wide field.

Nettles tall as a small man made a stinging jungle on each side of the path and you had to run with care if you didn't want blisters for badges. We scrambled across the fence into the field and flew over the short grass, over the golden dandelions, into the morning and the winds of the morning where the silver hazel woods were, and the tilted meadows with their sleepless saxophonist corncrakes.

The chestnut candles were burning too when Ulick's parents died within a week of each other and he went off to live with his Aunt in England. Sixteen years old he was, and I watched the train until its whistle, as it rounded the shoulder of Tubber Mountain, sent a litter of little lonely echoes scurrying through the Glen. The months melted down the candles into brown blobs of nuts, the cold winds blew from the sea but Ulick never wrote. The years piled up like dead leaves and he never came home. In the Glen where he was loved people wondered at the silence.

'Stranger than a white blackbird how Ulick Donoghue never came home,' they said. 'He's too busy putting them on their edges, I suppose. Ay, wherever that lad is he's getting on well for there was something to him.'

But from the world beyond the bog there came no news of Ulick to satisfy their curiosity.

It is the tradition of the Glen that all its young men leave it for a while ... or for ever. When I was twenty-one I went to America and worked in the big automobile factory in Detroit. In the killing heat of the American June the chestnut tree in the Glen jumped across the world and thrust its roots deep in my mind and I could see the white candle-blossoms flaming above my head. With it came Ulick, running barefooted through the long grass or shouting among the furze bushes on the mountain while the grass-hoppers were everywhere, making their webs of music across the rocks. Ten years of my life I gave to American industry. I decided that the Glen should have the remainder, be it long or short. I booked my passage home for Christmas and took the train to New York.

I had some hours to spare before the boat sailed and I turned into a saloon for a drink to while away the time. I was sitting at a table when a door marked 'Private' opened and two men entered. One of them, who was in his shirt-sleeves, I judged to be the owner of the place, and the other was a well-dressed man of my own age. They shook hands as I watched. The saloon-keeper disappeared behind the door marked 'Private' and his companion began to walk swiftly towards the exit. As he was passing my table I caught his eye, smiled and said casually: 'Hello, Ulick'.

He stiffened in his tracks and stared at me.

'I don't think I know you, Bud. Do I?' he said.

'You did once upon a time,' I told him.

'I meet so many people,' he apologised. 'You're Irish, of course?'

'Better than that, Ulick; I spent a lot of my youth with you. Do you remember the chestnut tree in the Glen?'

His eyes widened and he flopped into a chair beside me.

'Tadgh Cantillon! Not Tadgheen himself surely?'

'The very same, Ulick. We climbed to the top of the old Mill together, and Daniel O'Connell's tree, and the high ash in Primrose where the herons had their nest. Remember?'

'Sure, I remember. Boy, boy, how you bring it all back to me.'

There was a queer strained sadness in his eyes as he looked at me.

'I'm going back to the Glen by tonight's boat,' I told him. 'Been working in Detroit these past ten years and I can't stand it any longer. By the way, I didn't ask you to have a drink. Name it.'

He waved aside my offer with an imperious hand. 'You'll pay for no drinks while I'm around. It's my party tonight, brother Cantillon.'

I remembered how he used always issue the orders when we were kids and I smiled. He flung a $10 bill on the table and beckoned a barman.

'They're wondering in the Glen whether you're dead or alive,' I told him.

'Sure, I'm alive. Why wouldn't I? I have a lot to live for.'

'They always said that you'd get on, Ulick.'

'Sure, I got on, Tadgh. I've got two saloons on the other side of the river. One of them would make four of this joint. When I met you I was on my way to negotiate a deal for a third one. Sure, I did OK for myself.'

'They'll be glad to hear of your success at home. It isn't often one of us makes the grade.'

He laughed amusedly, as though making a fortune was as easy as cutting furze bushes.

'You know how the saying goes, Tadgheen. Some people build houses for other people to live in. I left England when I was seventeen and I've been here ever since. To get on in this country you got to be a go-getter.'

'Maybe you'll pay the old country a visit some time soon, Ulick?'

'I'm all tied up for a year or two, but I would like to see that old chestnut tree again. You know, Tadgh, there's something I've always regretted. That I didn't carve my name on that old tree-trunk. So the people would remember me when they saw it.'

'I'll carve it for you when I get back,' I told him.

'Sure, Tadgh, do it for me. Slice Ulick Donoghue out of that old trunk and send me a snap of it.'

The barman came with the drinks and we drank and conversed together until a sudden glance at my watch told me it was time to move. We arose and went out together into the street. He shook my hand fiercely when we parted.

'Don't forget to tell the folks way back home that Ulick Donoghue isn't in his bare feet any longer.'

'I'll tell them you own half New York, Ulick.'

'Well, not exactly half. Say just a few of its goldmines.'

When he was gone I remembered he hadn't given me his address, but it occurred to me that a letter addressed 'Ulick Donoghue, New York,' would find him easily enough. However, I went back to the saloon to get his address. The proprietor was behind the counter and I beckoned him.

'Could you give me the address of one of Ulick Donoghue's saloons across the river?' I asked him.

He stared at me silently for a moment.

'One of his saloons, did you say, brother?'

'Yes, any one of them will do. He has two, hasn't he?'

He called to the barman nearest him.

'Say, Joe, what do you think of that? This guy tells me Donoghue owns two saloons across the river.'

'Well, what do you know!' exclaimed the barman, astonished.

The saloon-keeper leaned towards me confidentially.

'Listen, brother. Eleven years ago Donoghue and I worked together in a cannery in Chicago and he has never let me forget it. He's a no-good. Couldn't keep a job longer than a month. Tonight I gave him a suit of clothes and a $10 bill to help him along. That guy is no good, mister. Just white trash, brother. Just white trash.'

I hurried out of the saloon before he could tell me any more.

10. Blood

Before Aeneas MacCarthy had reached the age of fifteen, the parish of Trugreine realised that he had a future.

'He's as cute as a bee with a red car,' the people maintained, observing how he worked his way into the good graces of the gentry, holding their horses' heads, or opening the doors of the coaches and making himself useful to them in a thousand ways while the other boys, remembering their history, remained inimically aloof, or smashed each other's hurleys in the Mill field.

On his seventeenth birthday, Aeneas found himself apprenticed to Mr Wilson, the solicitor who had always taken more than a passing interest in him. He adapted himself to his new glory as though he had been born with a quill pen behind his ear. He began to wear black clothes, got used to having his feet encased in boots all the day, and coaxed a crease into his unruly hair. The transformation was so great that Mike Tom Brady, paying a visit to the solicitor on a matter of some importance, blinked when he saw him.

'And who might you be now?' asked Mike.

'I'm Mister MacCarthy, Wilson's clerk,' said Aeneas.

The story went through the countryside with the speed of a mackerel and when the people met Aeneas on the road they touched their forelocks in mock gravity and said, "Tis a fine day Mr MacCarthy,' or "Twill likely rain soon, Mr MacCarthy.'

Aeneas inclined his head to them in a superior sort of way after the fashion of the gentry, and proceeded.

From being an efficient clerk Aeneas passed on to be a brilliant solicitor. The other solicitors who were English-educated didn't know Irish and thought they knew the people, Aeneas knew both and besides, had more law in the lobe of his ear than the magistrates had in the rounds of their skulls.

Aeneas grew popular with the people and prospered. Once, when he won an important case against the crown, they harnessed themselves to his carriage and pulled him in triumph to his home. When he went to reside in the Big House, the mountains ran red with bonfires to celebrate a Cromwellian gone from the land and a MacCarthy come into his own. The ashes of the fires were scarcely cold when the crown offered to make him a magistrate, and he accepted because he thought it would influence his Big House neighbours to acknowledge him. But the Sucklings, the Pidgeons and the Perrotts continued to look askance and would have none of him. To them, he still was a barefoot native boy who opened the coach-doors for their fathers and helped their mothers across the muddy places. They killed their foxes, shot their grouse and woodcock, held their soirees but invited him not. In the gigantic emptiness of his Big House, he sat alone and learned to hate them all.

It was Biddy the Bag, a beggar woman who looked as though she had all the secrets of this world and the next hidden behind her bright beady eyes, handed him the notion that he had royal blood in his veins. He met her while walking the road beside his residence one day, and slipped a crown into her wrinkled palm.

'God's blessing on you, master, root and branch of the line of MacCarthy Mor, King of Munster,' she called after him.

He stopped dead and turned to her.

'Are you making a king out of me now, Biddy?' he laughed.

'If blood makes a man a king, master, you have it,' she told him.

She gathered the surrounding mountains to her with a gesture of her horny hand.

'The son of the MacCarthy Mor fled from here when the Robbers came. I had it from my grandmother who had more knowledge under the black of her nail than all the scholars find in their printed books.'

Her bare feet pattered a few yards down the road and she stopped again.

'Seek the truth, master, an' you'll know the wisdom of Biddy the Bag.'

He went home, deciding to dismiss the whole thing as a beggarwoman's whine, but all that night it gnawed at his dreams like a mouse. The following day he wrote to Dublin to ascertain the rightful heir to the title of MacCarthy Mor and sent Flann Casey, Abigail's handyman husband, to the stage-coach with the letter. If it was true, he would put the Pidgeons, Sucklings and Perrotts in their places. He would legalise his title and paint his coat-of-arms on his coach. He would show the descendants of the scum of Cromwell's army, who refused to admit him, that it was time they acknowledged a superior. God! If it were only true....

Now he stood inside the window and watched the evening flood the bogs with a blue mist. The enpurpled mountains looked like gigantic piles of ripe plums. In the wood beside the house a ring dove tossed up little circles of sleepy sound that floated across to him on the still air.

'Michael,' he called to the gardener.

'Yes, sir?'

'Any sign of Casey with the mail?'

'He's coming up the drive, sir.'

He went outside the house to collect the letters. He skipped through them in search of the one he wanted most. He tore it open impatiently and glanced at it. A long collection of names and addresses with the vital information in the last paragraph.

'The rightful heir to the title of MacCarthy Mor would appear to be the eldest son of Eoin MacCarthy of Beenmore, in the parish of Trugreine, in the County of Kerry.'

He crushed the letter in his fist and looked across to where the gardener bent over his beloved strawberries.

'Michael!' he said.

'I'm coming, sir,' answered the gardener.

The crown magistrate remained stiff as a stone man and watched Black Michael, son of Eoin of Beenmore, direct descendant of MacCarthy Mor, King of Munster, walk towards him slowly.

11. Homecoming

Micka Boylan, deck-hand on the *ss Glendoag*, picked his way gingerly like a cat down the slippery gangplank and stood on the slushy quay. Above him the stars quivered and all about him the city lay hushed and swaddled in its cloak of snow. Winter in Cork. Midnight, star-light, snow white and biting cold.

He stood awhile listening to the white silence, feeling strangely queer as though he were the first man to land on the moon and fearful of what lay hidden in the shadowy corners. He was home again, back where he belonged in God's own town and the devil's own people, as the Kerryman in Jamaica had described it with that little touch of friendly malice that Kerrymen always use when talking of Cork.

Home again after twenty years of roving, and worse than roving. Back again to the lights of Pana and the cold whisper of the river Lee as it turned its glassy face to the twinkling stars.

He took a deep breath and then a killing cough gripped his chest with red-hot iron fingers. He fought the pain grimly until the torture died away. One of his lungs was gone and the other was as tender as tissue paper. Three months previously the doctors had given him half-a-year to live. That was why he had come back, just to feel the home ground under his feet before they piled some other ground over them.

The City Hall clock struck and he turned. Twelve strokes pounded the icy crispness of the night. The sound came towards him in throbbing widening waves until he fancied he felt the rims of them breaking against his body. Twelve o'clock! Home!

He turned right up a side street, then left and came to the centre of the city. The lamps, blobbed with snow, threw chequered patches of light on the white pavements. A couple of patrolling policemen saved the streets from being utterly deserted.

He crossed the river and climbed the hill until he came to Carroll Street. He moved along it dourly, watching the names of the houses until he found the one he sought. It was a draper's shop, glittering with goldleaf and prosperous with plate-glass. The big letters above the door told that it belonged to Cornelius Gallagher, High-Class Draper & Outfitter.

He stopped and stared at the name, his lips twisted bitterly. So Cornelius had made the grade after all. Just like he said he would. Well, he had been wise to stay on board the tramp during the daylight. Cornelius was the kind of man you always run into when you most wanted to avoid him. And he didn't want to meet Cornelius any more. No sir.

They had been in the Australian outback together, prospecting for gold, and one day the police found them. They didn't want Cornelius but they needed one John Graham for a five-year-old bank robbery. It wasn't his real name but in his lifetime he had used many such, and anyway he did a seven-year stretch for robbery under arms and he never saw Cornelius again.

'I know Cork like the palm of my hand, Graham,' Cornelius used to say. 'What part are you from?'

'Shandon Street,' he lied.

'I never knew any Grahams in Shandon Street,' said Cornelius, 'and I could run up and down either side of it and not miss a name.'

The fire burnt low and the aboriginal servant boy grunted in his sleep.

'I left Carroll Street with half-a-crown in my pocket. I'm not going back until I have enough to buy half of it up. If ever you're in Cork, Graham, look out for my name in

Carroll Street.' Thus Cornelius counted his dreams beside the fire in the Australian bush...

Boylan stared at the glittering shop and smiled ruefully. When the police had arrested him, he had given over his gear and grub-stake to his partner. He wondered if Cornelius had struck it rich then, while the damp jail played havoc with his lungs. He shrugged his shoulders and moved away, his shoes switching twin paths through the snow.

The houses on either side were still awake as he walked up Horse Lane. He stopped in front of the last house on his right. The door was ajar and he could hear the voices of women. He knocked and pushed the door open, and entered. His mother sat in the arm-chair before the fire, two sticks resting against her skirt. She was old, very old. He removed his cap and stood there watching her. She stared blankly back at him, saying nothing. His sister arose and came towards him.

'What is it you want, sir?' she asked. She didn't know him, and his mother didn't know him. He saw his face in the big mirror above the fireplace and he knew it would be hard for anybody to recognise him. His face was scarred from forehead to chin.

The knife of the Lascar who ran amok in Bombay had done that to him ten years previously. Galloping consumption was doing its worst with those parts of his face left unmarked by the Lascar's knife. Yes, it would be hard for anyone to recognise him. He hardly recognised himself.

'My name is John Graham,' he told his sister. 'I'm looking for Mrs Boylan. I was directed here.'

'I'm Mrs Boylan,' said his mother. 'Won't you sit down?'

He sat opposite her.

'You gave me a start,' she said, 'I thought at first you were Micka.'

'I've come from Micka,' he told her.

She looked at him with very old, very wise eyes.

'He's dead, isn't he?' she asked simply.

He nodded.

'Six months ago in Port Said of fever.'

His sister began to weep softly.

'Poor Micka. He was always the wild one. The big world itself was too small for Micka,' whispered his mother.

'He gave me some money for you,' he said, but she didn't hear him. She kept on talking to herself as though he wasn't there at all.

'So he died of fever. Poor Micka. He was so strong I thought if the mountains fell on him they wouldn't kill him.'

'Poor Micka, God be good to him.'

His sister came to him wiping her eyes.

'She's very old,' she said. 'Her mind wanders a lot.'

He took out his wallet and put it on his mother's lap. 'There's £100 in it, Micka said to tell ye it was come by honestly,' he told his sister.

He rose and put on his cap.

'I must go now, ma'am. My ship sails with the tide.'

At the door he turned. His mother was still gazing at the fire and talking about Micka, the wallet lying unopened in her lap. He looked at his sister.

'Goodbye,' he said.

He closed the door behind him and walked down the lane and came out on the street. Beneath him he could see the floor of the city sparkling like a plate of jewels. Suddenly the clock on the Shandon began to strike, releasing fluttering butterflies of sound that seemed to brush his face as they flew past. One by one the other clocks chimed the hour until the whole city was a bowl of splendid music under the twinkling toes of the stars.

12. The Memorial

I was sitting among the furze on the bounds ditch, smoking my pipe and watching the crows sprinting down the evening sky when I saw the man in American clothes coming up the road. He was a stranger to me, lean, lightfoot, fiftyish, I judged, though you can never rightly tell with Yanks the way they carry themselves. When he came near he waved as though I had sent a cablegram for him, and took off the wide grey hat to wallop the midges away from the bridge of his nose.

'Your insects don't like strangers, I guess,' he said as he sat down beside me.

'They don't see many strangers here,' I told him, 'and no doubt the change of diet does them good.'

He was a fine friendly man right enough and after half-an-hour's chat I learned more concerning him than I knew about myself. He was American-born but his father, who had arrived in New York as a boy, was Irish to the backbone and had talked so much about the Old Country that he came to regard it as a second home.

'About a year after Pop died,' said the Yank, 'I went to visit his grave. I thought there would surely be a carpet of shamrocks on it and do you know what I found growing there? A rose. The red of England. Gee, if only Pop knew that!'

'It would have killed him,' I said and we both laughed at my little joke.

'I passed the remains of an old house beside the mill on my way up,' he said, 'Looked as though it was the end of a happy story or the beginning of a sad one.'

'That's where Denis Hayden lived,' I enlightened him and then I had to put flesh on the bones for him and give him the whole body.

Denis and his widowed mother farmed a few acres beside the river in the bad old days and were snug enough until Sam Arnold, the landlord, thought the lad didn't touch his forelock as respectfully as he should whenever he met him on the road. He evicted them when the rains of winter were falling, and threatened to evict anybody that gave them shelter as well.

The old woman went off to the workhouse and one night, a week afterwards, a masked man held up Sam Arnold's coach and shot him dead. Sam's driver, Paddy the Coach, said he recognised Denis though the night was as black as the pot, and the police scoured the country for him. He was arrested taking the ship to America at Cove Harbour, tried, sentenced and hanged in Cork.

The Yank was deeply moved by my story. When I finished he shook his head sadly.

'Gee, they were terrible times,' he said. 'That poor boy hanged in the wrong and probably someone else did the shooting.'

'He was hanged in the wrong, all right,' I agreed, 'but he shot Sam Arnold right enough and 'twas the proper thing to do to the old tyrant.'

'Haven't ye erected any memorial to that brave boy?' he asked.

'I'm afraid we haven't,' I said.

'No memorial to a lad who gave his all to end tyranny. It's a shame. An almighty shame.'

He said 'so long' to me and walked smartly down the road towards the village. Then Dan Carmody, who had been watching the pair of us from the gable-end of his house, came across to me.

'Who's that fellow?' he asked.

'Some Yank,' I told him, 'that's wandering around writing a book about Ireland.'

Dan was an annoying brand of braggart. He talked about the Column leaders as though he had hand-reared them. If an ambush was being discussed 'twas Dan who advised the plan of campaign if 'twas a successful ambush. Then when you peered into Dan's real history you found the bosthoon had tiptoed away to the west whenever there was an ambush in the east. The same everywhere I suppose. The genuine keep quiet and the false never stop boasting.

One Saturday morning I got word to attend an important meeting in the schoolhouse that night. The Yank was there with most of the valley men around him. I noticed the figure covered with a cloth beneath the school clock.

'Gentlemen,' said the Yank, 'I guess you're all wondering why you've been asked to come here tonight. Well, the story begins with my friend, Mister O'Connell. It was he told me all about Denis Hayden.'

Everybody looked at me as though I had two heads on my shoulders.

'I learned from Mister O'Connell,' continued the Yank, 'that there was no memorial erected to the memory of this gallant boy, and it set me thinking. Well, gentlemen, thinking is one thing and action is another, so I commissioned the best sculptor in Ireland to chisel a memorial to Denis Hayden and here it is.'

He whipped off the cloth from the figure under the clock and we held our breaths at the beauty of it. It portrayed a young man with a pike kneeling while an old woman in a cloak gave him her blessing before he marched off into battle.

The Yank saw we liked it and he beamed with happiness.

'Gentlemen,' he said, 'your pleasure is my pleasure.'

Then Dan Carmody who was sitting in the front bench stood up and glared at the beaming Yank.

'Why wouldn't you?' he sneered, 'when 'twas your grandfather, Paddy the Coach, that put the rope about his neck.'

You could have heard a feather drop, for none of us knew the Yank's ancestry except Carmody.

The remark changed the Yank's face to a death-mask and there was a tremble in his voice when he spoke.

'Gentlemen, my little secret is out under the light. Sure my grandfather was Paddy the Coach, and it was exactly three years ago I learned the whole truth of his connection with the death of Denis Hayden. I came here to see your valley and this memorial is my tribute to a dead boy who suffered through one of my blood. Goodnight, gentlemen.'

He was out the door before we recovered our wits.

'Good riddance,' shouted Carmody and he'd have said more, only Tim Sheehy stood up and looked hard at him. Tim had as many wounds as a gladiator, but he never said very much and when he spoke you listened.

'Carmody,' said Tim, "tis people like you that were never any good have this world the way it is. Get out before I kick you over the mountain.'

We all, barring Dan, marched into the village but the Yank had left and we never saw him again. We stood the Denis Hayden Memorial in the middle of the village and we got Paddy Brien, the stone mason, to carve on it:

'Erected by a good Irishman,
Daniel M. O'Sullivan, of New York.'

We felt 'twas what Denis Hayden wanted us to do.

13. Randal's Ring

The river ran beside the old ash tree, its throat full of little tinkling bells, and the stones shouldered their way through the white lace of waters when the rain fell on the hills. The river talked to the tree as it sped past, telling it about the great salmon returning from the Atlantic to the lonely pools of their birth high up among the heather. Tales it told, too, for those who had the ears to understand of the whistling otter among the alders, the brown trout hiding his speckles against the pebbles, and the heron standing grave and watchful like a policeman where the pools were shallow. Two hundred years the ash tree had stood guard by the river when I first saw it.

Two roads ran by it. The grand main road, smooth as a worn six-pence, swaggered across the bridge and ribboned through the fields to Sealtown. The byroad, my favourite, ran beneath it to the river's brim. It was more a boreen than a road, floored with slippery stones and it leaked like a torn boot when the rains came. But when summer began it was a thing of beauty, throbbing with golden furze and milky hawthorn, and with the red breasts of robins lining the fences like Christmas cards.

I was standing in the middle of the boreen and taking my first look at the tree when a voice came out of the hawthorn bush beside me.

'There's a king buried under yonder tree,' the voice said.

I turned and saw a man sitting on the fence, his blackthorn stick stabbing at the ancient ash. He was a very old man, bearded like a druid, and wearing clothes belonging to a fashion even older than himself. He had very pale blue eyes, and his wet lips opened and closed continuously over his toothless gums.

'I remember well the night they buried him, for wasn't I at the funeral,' he continued.

'Was he a real king?' I asked, deciding that a man so old and so oddly clad should be humoured at all costs.

'No less a personage than the King of Munster himself,' he answered. 'Didn't they tell me so themselves!'

'They?' I queried.

He shook his head with the impatience of knowledgeable old age for an ignorant young lad of twelve.

'The dead heroes who buried him,' he explained. 'Kilted and cross-gartered they were like the pictures in the history book, and they carried spears and shields. Fine men they were, I tell you, seven feet high and as broad as a turf bank. 'Tis a pity to have their likes vanished from the land and leprechauns running around in the place of them.'

He spat venomously at the ground to show his contempt for anyone under seven feet, and beheaded an inoffensive fairy-fingers with his stick.

'Is it long since they buried the King of Munster?' I asked him.

'Ah, 'tis longer than yesterday anyway,' he said. 'I was a young man of thirty-five at the time and if the parish held one man as strong as me I assure you it didn't hold two. Coming across the hill there from my kinspeople in Dromarack I was and the darkness with me. 'Twas facing midnight when I came to the tree and I saw them. Twenty men or more, giants all of them and dressed like I told you. They had a grave dug under the roots of the tree and beside it they had the body of the king on a stretcher of hazel branches. I stood looking and I was clung to the ground until they buried him. Then the leader glared at me with his two burning eyes and he said, "The King of Munster himself is buried here. Whoever disturbs his rest will have a curse on him for ever".

'Then they all marched into the southern hills there and I saw no more of them.'

'Has nobody dug under the tree since?' I asked.

He switched his pale blue eyes on me as though I had insulted him.

'Who would have the courage to dig and the curse of the Fianna on it?' he growled.

I decided that it wouldn't be safe to pursue the subject any further. 'Do you live around here?' I asked.

He pointed to where a cabin humped on the lip of the byroad. It was a small, thatched, tramp's hat of a house, limewashed a dirty white, with one tiny window like a mouse's eye peering at the passing world.

'I didn't always live in the likes of that,' he assured me. 'I had a good farm once but I had a bad brother and he drank and gambled himself and myself out on the road.'

'Sometimes brothers are like that,' I said lamely.

'Lucifer himself would be a better brother to me than the same gentleman. A bit of a dandy he was, always wearing fine clothes and fancy watches and gold rings, and spending all his nights and most of his days in the porter-shops of Sealtown beyond. One night, just before we were to be evicted, he disappeared. He couldn't stand the shame of it, I suppose. He was talking about America a few days before and 'tis there he is, likely. Down the years he never wrote. Dead he is, I suppose, like a good many more.'

His face was wistful like a man thumbing through the pictures of his vanished children, and I was sorry for him. I said goodbye and moved up the road towards Sealtown.

He called after me.

'Tell your father there's a king buried under the tree and a curse will fall on the hand that disturbs his bones.'

I turned around in surprise but he was shuffling out of sight among the river's bushes.

My father was the county council's engineer, and we had only been living for three weeks in the neighbourhood. It was a fast piece of work on the part of my seanchaí friend to know who I was. Still anything could be possible to a man who was at the midnight burial of a king and who got good advice from the Fianna.

When I arrived home I repeated the old man's warning to my father who had enough cynicism in him to flatten the pyramids.

'What does he think his tree is? King Tut's Tomb or something? The old boy must have got the wind of tomorrow's big bang,' he said.

'What big bang?' I asked him.

'That tree overhangs the main road and is a danger to passing traffic. The trunk is beginning to rot and the first big wind would bowl it over and have somebody killed. I'm shoving a few sticks of gelignite under it tomorrow, and the king can start cursing as soon as he likes.'

'I wonder is there really a king buried there?' I asked.

My father gave me a look that would wither grass.

'We're not that short of graveyards, son,' he told me. 'Griffin, the road steward was telling me about your seanchaí friend. He's as mad as a hatter. His name is Mickey Randal and in his youth he was a decent hardworking fellow. He had a ruffian of a brother known as Denis the Dandy who used to roll home at night from the taverns and hammer poor Mickey unmercifully. He drank them both into poverty and then disappeared to America. Mickey has never been the same man since he went away, although one would imagine he was well rid of the scoundrel.'

'And tomorrow the tree comes down, father,' I said.

'That's right,' he said. 'Tomorrow we'll blow Mickey's yarn about kings and curses skyhigh.'

The following day quite a crowd of people gathered to see the ancient ash being destroyed. The sticks of gelignite were inserted and we stood back beside the river. We were joined by old Mickey who gazed sadly at my father.

'I hear you're levelling the king's tree,' he said.

'I am, Mickey,' my father told him, 'before it falls of its own accord and kills somebody.'

'The king won't like it,' Mickey said.

'He'll have to get used to it,' my father replied.

He raised his hand and lowered it almost immediately. There was a loud explosion and the tree shook and slowly toppled to the ground, while snapped branches cracked like rifle-shots. A cloud of dust hovered a while and slowly vanished. Then somebody shouted in a loud voice with fear in it.

'Look at the king!'

There, tangled among the torn roots, was a goodly portion of a human skeleton.

We stood and stared and the only one to speak was old Mickey.

'Didn't I tell ye not to interfere with the king's rest?' he wailed. 'Didn't I warn ye all in time?'

My father and the workmen gathered about the tree with hatchets and saws and began to cut up the stricken ash. My father started searching in the hole made by the uprooted tree. The on-lookers screwed their courage and drew closer, and I was by myself on the river's bank. After a while my father joined me.

'So old Mickey was right after all,' I said.

He opened his hand and I saw an earth-stained ring lying on his palm.

'Ancient kings didn't wear hall-marked gold rings,' he told me. 'I may be wrong, but I'd lay a big bet that this belonged to Denis the Dandy. It looks like he molested old Mickey once too often.'

We looked around for Mickey but he was walking along the river to his own cabin. My father shook his head and slipped the ring into his pocket.

'The perfect crime,' he said, 'if it was a crime. There's nobody around now to identify the ring.'

That night old Mickey died in his sleep, and the day after the funeral we went away from Sealtown.

I have never been back there since.

14. Home to my Mountain

Lying back in the hot sun, I am on the furzey slope of Beenathee Mountain, with all the glen beneath me, and the town in the middle of it, the dead spit of a catapult tossed down on the green fields by some careless giant.

Strange it is that I never before realised how like a catapult our town is, with the handle of Fenian Street flowing towards the gap in the eastern mountains, and Market and Mail Coach Streets making a fork that prod the sea and the western islands. Or, maybe, it isn't strange at all, with so many more exciting things to beguile the youthful eye, the blue-grey wings of a heron breast-stroking laboriously towards the river, a hawk nailed to the roof of the sky, the skiing water-spiders in the well under the hazel bushes, a stoat, relentless as a process server, on the trail of a trembling rabbit...

There is a tickling on the calf of my leg and I pulled my trousers to examine it. A ladybird it is, moving about, spotted shoulders humped, head scraping my skin, like a shortsighted boy reading his lessons. I take it in my hand and blow it gently. The shining body sprouts wings as though an invisible fairy wand had touched it, and it flies away among the furze. I watch it until distance blacks out the rich redness of the shell.

One hundred yards beneath me is the Rocky Road. Every stone on it I know for every stone on it I love. Queer it is how one road out of a thousand loops itself about your heart and you must see it every day to be happy, like a lovesick man and his sweetheart.

Patie Andy, the last of the old huntsmen, comes up the road, his five beagles weaving in front of him. Comely, Juno, Coleen, Ceolawn, Melody they're called, names tasselled with little silver bells. I watch him until the white throat of the hawthorn swallows him.

I remember how we used to go hunting with him on the mountains when we were wild young blades, before the great scattering came, and the old pain flickers in me like a flame. Sweet were the hounds of yesterday in the high hills tolling.

Opposite me a wedge of sea splits a good four miles of the glen, and spanning it is the railway bridge with its stout, strong, tug-o-war team's legs firm against the pull of the current.

The bridge breaks into thunder as the half-two train crosses it and struggles up by the Mountain of the Wells, puffing frantically like an old man in a hurry. The train reaches the Gap and its triumphant whistle awakes triumphant echoes among the rocks. Beyond the Gap it is downhill all the way to Killarney town.

The slope drags the last carriage out of sight and my eyes slip sideways to the river.

Empty must the boyhood be that hasn't a river running through it. Before and after school we haunted it when the water tossed white heels at the willows, or when it flowed smooth and brown with the gentle murmur of it sending sleep into the head. Lie on the banks for hours we would, watching the rounded amber pebbles winking at the sun, or the spotted trout slipping over the stones, or the little eels losing their way among the thin green weeds.

Or in the lonely reaches of the river we would dive in, naked as a leaf, and swim about in the cool water, like young carefree otters.

Sometimes we would discover Michael, the trapper, crouched among the bushes, immobile as a Budda, for he had the gift of remaining still for hours. When he saw we had nosed him out he would gather up his cages and go home for no charm of goldfinches would allow him to share a parish with us let alone the thistle-field by the river.

And we would continue on our way, trailing the river through the fields, across the brown bog and up the mountain to the dark lake that gave it birth. Bottomless they say the lake is and with a monster in its depths who comes to the surface on a night of full moon. Eerie it looked by day, too, so that we shivered and waited a while before we dashed down the mountain to where the willows and hazels elbowed each other along the warm river-banks, and the king-fisher flashed his rainbow by the water's edge.

Sweet river, flow softly for our youth is gone.

15. Tryst

I am lounging with my back to the Commander's Corner among the other fellows and keeping an eye on the lamp across the street in case Mary Grant passes under it. She's the new servant girl with Mrs Tom Nolan, the baker, a tall lightfoot lass with strange blue eyes and a head of black curls so tight they might have come off knitting needles. I saw her the first day she came, a week ago Monday, and her face is haunting me all the time like the banshee haunts my mother's people, if you can believe them.

I saw Mary on the street yesterday and I gave her the eye but she passed me as though I was a process-server hunting down her father. 'Tisn't the kind of treatment I usually get from girls I bend an eye on but then she's different. You can see by those neat ankles that she's a thoroughbred. None of your pick me up and leave me where you found me business with her. I got it bad this time, right enough.

A cold night for January, with frost polishing the stars as we huddle closer to the Corner away from the teeth of the wind. We are not real corner boys, understand. It's just that we don't drink and we can only work when the mackerel-shoals hit the coast, and they always stay somewhere warmer for the winter. And who's to blame them, indeed. Come spring and the Corner will be bare enough for when you've spent the day from six in the morning, cutting, gutting and salting mackerel it's into a bed you'll fall even one mattressed with barbed wire and quilted with broken bottles, and suffer no insomnia either.

The lads around me are arguing about champion greyhounds and as I know nothing concerning the animals I decide to escape. I look around for Jimmy Connell to tell him we'll hop along to Donovan's to see the old men playing cards and bickering like starlings when one of them makes a hash of things. I look harder but there's no sign of Jimmy which is passing peculiar seeing how we both came to the Corner together ten minutes before.

'See Jimmy?' I ask Padder Casey.

'Saw him slipping around by the forge a few minutes ago when he thought there was nobody looking,' Casey tells me.

I skip it to the forge and see Jimmy's straight back melting into the darkness. The road that way is quiet and lonely, and there are no lamps to it. Strange him slipping away like that without telling me as though I'm some kind of informer for Jimmy is my best friend and it hurts. I stand a while looking and then decide to follow him and see what his game is.

Jimmy and myself are closer to each other than briars to blackberries, and have been ever since we robbed our first orchard together. We work shoulder to shoulder in the same fish-curing shed. When I wheel my bike out of the house at half-five in the morning, Jimmy is there before me with his boot on the pedal ready to jump into his saddle. Sundays find us together walking the mountains, listening to the rocks give back-chat to the beagles belling among the heather.

He's a quiet one preferring to listen than talk which suits me as I'm a bit of a chatterer myself. Cigarettes or girls don't mean a thing to him and he's always been so dependent on me it annoys me now like a heel-blister to see him dimly in the darkness ahead of me, snaking off without a word.

The road loops to the left and joins hands with a narrow lane that the back-yards of the Main Street shops run into. When I reach the bend I round it cautiously and find Jimmy has vanished like a ghost at cockcrow. I stand there wondering and then smile as the answer comes to me. The gate of Hogan's pub is open and it is the custom of the lads who are learning to down a bottle of stout to enter the local taverns by the back doors and drink in the kitchens until they've passed the apprentice stage. The bould Jimmy is growing up in spite of me — and passing me out at that. I think I'll let him grow up in peace for tonight at any rate. I move up the lane and then as I see the lighted kitchen of Baker Nolan's my heart nearly stops. I stand watching it thinking of Mary Grant until my feet tell me to walk or freeze to death. I decide to take one peep through the window and see Mary in her own kingdom before I go home to dream about her. As I tiptoe up the yard I can hear the chatter from the upstairs sittingroom where the Nolans are entertaining friends. I reach the window and peep in.

Mary is there, lovely enough to own half the town, sitting beside the fire with a cup of tea in her hand. She is with somebody and I move to the far side of the window to see who it is. My eyes nearly fall out on me. Jimmy is sitting on the other side as smug as if the turf came out of his bog, a cup of tea by him and a plate of cake balanced on his knee. He's chattering away like a stream, a big smile on his foolish face, and Mary's looking at him the way I dream she looks at me. The more I watch the dog with his Mary and his cake and his comfort the more I hate him.

I move back from the kitchen, pick up a hefty stone and peg it at the window. There is a crash of glass like an iceberg being dynamited. Jimmy and Mary get to their feet too surprised to do anything except stare, and they are still that way when Tom Nolan and his wife come pounding in on them.

I tiptoe swiftly out of the backyard and let Jimmy do the talking.

16. Something for the Wran

On St Stephen's Day I was out of bed as early as an engine-driver and peering down at the town to see if the chimneys had reddened their pipes for the morning smoke. Plumes rising here and there, faith, to keep my heart in good fettle, for I had been visited by a terrible distressing dream during the night, which told me that all the Main Street people had died in their beds and the wran was abolished. Real enough that dream was to have the smell of black crepe in my nostrils and not a penny in my pocket to bury them, for there was no one left alive in the town except myself and Mike Shea, the baker. A relief, then, to find they were still lively and not gone away on me and the chance of bullion gone with them.

Down with the breakfast as if I was a wolf after a hunger-strike, out the door, and along the street with a frost-polished face, where a Birnam Wood of holly bushes was already roving up and down searching for a Dunsinane with coppers in it. Every ribbony bush was sharply inspected, for the fellow who boasted a wran in his holly was a hero in a regiment of batmen. Nobody had a wran and everybody was pleased, for heroes weren't too popular in our army.

I had a bird cut out of a spud with a few feathers stuck in him to give him a plumey appearance. Ugly enough to frighten a hawk into becoming a vegetarian he was for there were no artistic carvers in my ancestry or I'd have heard the boasting before now. Bob Doyle had a brahareen (hedge-sparrow in the Beurla) that he found dead in the frost to rise the envy in us slightly for a brahareen was only in the dunces' class compared with a wran. Tommy Boland had a birdeen with the colours of the rainbow in his feathers and we nearly sank our teeth in the calf of his leg when we recognised it.

'That's a stuffed bird you stole out of the glass case in school,' we accused him.

'I only took the loan of it,' Tommy said. 'I'll put it back tomorrow.'

Mad we were we didn't think of it ourselves. And I wouldn't mind, only the thief made a fortune with it.

We marched along from door to door singing the oldest begging-song in the world.

> The wran, the wran, the king of all birds,
> I broke his skull in Jer Donoghue's furze.
> Up with the kittle and down with the tay,
> Give me a copper and let me away.

If it was an Irish-speaking door, and plenty of them in the town then, we cut the other side of the record with a green, white and yellow needle.

> Dreoilin a fuaireas-sa thios i Bheul Inse
> (A wran I captured below in Valentia)
> Fe bhraid carraige agus carabhat sioda air.
> (Under a rock a silken cravat on him).

Bilingual scamps with money-minds we were and all the richer for it in brown coppers when the day was done.

Norrie Hyland, an elderly spinster home to us from Boston, had the door closed and no sign of it opening if I was knocking yet. I peeped in the keyhole to make sure she hadn't dropped dead on us, for she lived alone without even a pussy cat for company. My faith in the generosity of returned Yanks was splintered severely when I saw her on her tippy-toes around the kitchen like a Willy Wagtail.

'That's the last gallon of water I'll carry for you from Mike Healy's well,' I promised her in the quietness of my mind, and I ran into Mrs Doney, the Bread, next door, where three pennies fresh and shining from the money-makers in London were waiting to dive into my pocket. A cousin to my mother Mrs Doney was, and making sure I had the sweet word in my mouth for her when I reached home, for she only gave a few worn ha'pennies to the fellows coming hot on my heels.

Four doors away my grandfather's Stephen Day shakehands always had a silver sixpence in it. He was sitting on the edge of his sugawn chair beside the fire with a whip in his hand for all the world as if he was behind a pair of spanking greys, driving the mail car to Killarney.

'Did you clap an eye at all on that bosthoon son of Biddy Brazil around with the wran?' he asked.

'He's coming down the street now, Daddo,' I told him.

Then I remembered how Paudeen Brazil had tossed a dead hen in my grandfather's door the week before. The fact that I was scoundrel enough to put Paudeen up to doing the deed was neither here nor there, once my grandpa didn't know it, and I ran out on the street to encourage him to call.

'Daddo is running out of coppers,' I told him, 'You better hurry if you want a lop, boy.'

Paudeen's right eye examined me as though I was advising him to invest his money in making fur coats for Polar bears or water-wings for sea-lions. The vigorous, rigorous way of life among the youth of Mill Road had taught him not alone to look before he leaped but to have a photograph of the place taken and carefully studied before he removed his boots for the jump. It was the survival of the slickest, and if that yardstick measured longevity correctly Paudeen was likely to live to one hundred and ten in any zone, temperate, frigid or torrid.

'Has he forgotten about the hen you told me throw in the door to him?' he asked.

'He didn't say a word about it,' I told him, which was true enough, in the letter if not in the spirit.

I had no remorse about not warning him, for Puadeen would have cut the cloth for me to a similar size. Indeed, he would have pushed me in and pulled the door shut behind me, and given the world afterwards a mirthy description of the corrective treatment, wallop by wallop.

He approached the door as warily as a process-server with a summons for a moonlighter, and cocked his head sideways to survey all corners.

'Something for the wran,' he sang out, and that was the note he nearly perished on. Daddo came from behind the dresser like a step-dancer and the whip made a snake-leap for Paudeen's legs, only Paudeen wasn't standing there any longer. He fled down the street, hardly able to run under the weight of chuckles, and Daddo after him with the whip firing shots that never reached the target. We all began to cheer Daddo, and Paudeen was so delighted with the chase and the publicity that he'd likely throw a dead donkey in my grandfather's door before the New Year was well aired.

Beyond the pump that always ran dry after a week of fine weather, I saw Mike Shea, the baker, smoking his pipe, and I ran to talk to him.

'Mike,' I told him, 'I dreamt about you last night and everybody in the place was dead only the two of us.'

If we liked our elders we called them by their Christian names, which they didn't seem to mind, and if we didn't we mistered them.

Mike took the pipe from his mouth and eyed me gravely.

'It must be all the flat porter you drank,' he decided.

'Only lemonade I had, Mike,' I assured him.

'Ah then, it must be all the turkey you ate, Boy Bawn,' he said.

'We hadn't any turkey,' by myself, betraying the family table. 'A goose we had instead.'

'It must be the stuffing so,' he said. 'Here's tuppence and don't be cracking your skull with them queer dreams any more.'

Round the corner then and into Fenian Street. Knock, knock, knock on the doors, and every knock a song and every song a copper.

'Where's your wran, Boyeen?' Pat Driscoll, the butcher asked.

'There he is, Pat,' and I pointed out my treasure.

'Well, bless me anyway,' he said, 'but that wran would grow more stalks than feathers, if he was properly manured. Here's the price of a bow and arrow for you so you'll have a real wran for next Stephen's Day.'

The convent was always a last great feast of call, provided you hadn't a real bird in the cage of your holly. A long wedge of raisiny cake you'd get from Sister Bride and it thick enough to beat a donkey out of a sandpit. That was the hour of munching with a bottle of the best lemonade to wash it down in Miss Kinsella's shop, where the bell tinkled in the customers through the opening door. Home, then, to count your money and it burning a hole in your pocket for a day or two, until it was gone the way money should go keeping the ever-hungry jaws of the young in perpetual motion.

17. The Four Magpies

When the big foxy cat saw the donkey and cart outside the door and Old Tim reddening his pipe for the road he knew his master was going to the village and he'd be alone until nightfall. When the mood took himself he slipped away from the house for the length of a week without as much as a by-your-leave but he kicked up an almighty fuss whenever Tim left him alone for even half-a-day.

After the fashion of people who live by themselves in lonely places Tim always talked to his cat as if he was human.

'I'll be back before dark, I tell you, and I'll buy a few mackerel for you from Seamuseen O. Will that satisfy you, now?'

The cat steered the schooner-mast of his tail between Tim's legs and miaowed fiercely.

''Tisn't that you deserve mackerel, you lazy scoundrel. The house ate with mice and you're doing nothing about it. I declare to Jericho if the mice formed a pipers' band you'd march at the head of it carrying the banner instead of gobbling them up, whatever seed or breed of cats you're sprung from, you scamp.'

The cat followed Tim to where the boreen melted into the grandeur of the main road, and perched on the fence looking after him and crying as though he smelt the end of the world coming across the mountain. He stood there wailing until the cart rattled around a bend in the road and then curled up under a furze bush and fell asleep.

Beyond the Three Eye Bridge, Tim heard a chuckle in the air and looked up. It was a magpie making a movable black and white patch on the tent of the sky.

'One for luck,' said Tim. 'That's a good start to the day anyhow.'

A second magpie leaped up from the field behind the river and climbed to meet the first.

'Two for joy,' said old Tim, 'That's better again, faith.'

Half a mile further on in the Dean's field he saw a third magpie perched on a cow's back like a cheeky jockey.

'Three to get married,' quoted Tim. 'What do you think of that for advice, Barney?'

The donkey threw up his head meaning to say they were better off as they were with no woman flinging orders about her like oats to goslings.

'Begor,' said Tim, 'there's no sense in tackling at seventy-five what you were afraid of at twenty-one. Three to get married, fine girl you are!'

The words of an old ballad, about a damsel who lived on the mountains and whose stockings were white, ran into his mind and he began to sing them softly to shorten the journey. At the outskirts of the village he saw Razor Sullivan's small son, Daneen, standing beside his gate.

'Hello, Tim,' the boy said, 'I'll give you three guesses as to what I have behind my back.'

Tim halted the donkey, pursed his lips, and wrinkled his forehead to add importance to the occasion.

'Is it Finn MacCool's magic razor that was sharp enough to shave a mouse asleep?'

'No, no,' Daneen cried with delight. 'Guess again, Tim.'

'Is it the eye of the King of the Fomoricans that could see around corners?'

'You're miles out, Tim. Guess again.'

'Then it must be the golden angel that flew off with the Rock of Cashel last week.'

The boy whooped with delight at his victory, and showed him the young magpie he had hidden behind his back.

'I found him in the wood and I'm going to make a pet of him and, maybe, teach him to talk,' said the boy.

The magpie said nothing but eyed Tim as though he was measuring him for a coffin.

The old man drove into the village, the jingle about the magpies nagging at his brain. Four to die, the last line of it ran. He felt as healthy as a herring, but then it wasn't the sick ones who went all the time. Patch Fitzmaurice saw four magpies before he died a year ago and he was never a day sick in his life.

By the time he drew level with the chapel he decided to make his will without further delay. The village was too small to support a solicitor but Patrick Monahan who kept the hardware shop would oblige him. He tied the donkey to the pole outside the window, went in and whispered his business to Monahan who sat him in the parlour while he fetched pen and paper.

'I'll have to make my mark, Mr Monahan, for I can't read or write. My father, God rest him, didn't trouble to make a scholar out of me,' said Tim.

Mr Monahan smiled under his small foxy moustache and filled his fountain-pen.

'Education can have its drawbacks, too, Tim,' he replied. He didn't say what the drawbacks were.

The will was a simple matter. Tim had £500 in the post office, one acre of land, a house and a cat. With the exception of £20 for Masses he left everything to his favourite niece, Abigail Falvey, on condition that she looked after his cat. The will was witnessed by Monahan's two servant-girls. Tim gave him a pound for his trouble and went out to his donkey.

Further up the street he ran into his neighbour, James Donnelly. James had a scowl on his face that stretched from the peak of his cap to the knot of his tie.

'What's worrying you now, James?' he asked.

'It's my Aunt Mary's will,' replied Donnelly. 'There's going to be law over it and by the time we're through with the courts there won't be a shilling in the kitty. That eegit, Monahan, made a mess of the will when he was drawing it up.'

'Did he, faith!' said Tim, trying to look unconcerned.

When James was gone he sat in the cart thinking about his own will and wondering what he should do. He saw Father O'Carroll going in the chapel gate and he hurried after him. He took the will from his pocket and handed it to him.

'It's my will, Father. I'd be deeply obliged if you'd take a look at it and see if 'tis in order. You see, I can't read or write.'

Father O'Carroll read the will.

'Yes, it seems to be quite in order. You've left everything to your niece, Abigail Falvey, with the exception of £20 for Masses and £50 to your good friend, Patrick Monahan.'

Tim thanked him and took back the will. As he walked towards the street he tore it into little pieces and made a ball of it in the heel of his fist. He returned to Monahan's shop and went in the door. Monahan came to serve him with a £50 smile under his moustache.

'I've run short of money,' Tim explained, 'and I was wondering if you could lend me a pound until the next time I'm in the village.'

'Certainly, Tim, and ten of them,' said Monahan.

'One will do,' Tim told him. 'I hate owing too much money.'

He went out the door and didn't bother to look back.

MORE MERCIER BESTSELLERS

BALLADS OF A BOGMAN

Sigerson Clifford

Almost invariably Sigerson Clifford has set his word pictures against the mountain backdrop that edges Dingle Bay from the Laune to the Inney. To visit his Kerry is to go with him along the heathery pathways above Cahirciveen, or to sit with him in the cosy pub at The Point while the long ferryboat noses out from The Island. With a rare sense of intimacy he will take you, on bare feet through the dew-wet grass of sloping fields before the morning sun tops the shoulder of one of his mountains, or set you down in the scent of smouldering turf under, low rafters as darkly brown as the stout in your glass. In these ballads Sigerson Clifford has caught and held the witchery of Kerry.

The verses, wistful and gay, recall the comings and goings of a people whose limewhitened houses nestle in the hills between the bog and the lighthouse. The author has a true gift for ballad poetry. The tricks and turns of speech and thought that mark his work are delightful because they are so natural. And his eye for nature is as keen as a hawk's

BLESS ME FATHER

Eamon Kelly

Eamon Kelly is an excellent antidote to those dreary people among us who cannot see beyond the mists and loneliness and the pieties. They forget that there is a positive side too–energetic and ribald and, above all, gay. 'And gaeity is the hallmark of high intelligence.'

Wit, humour, a delicious turn of phase and a very unique sense of fun is on every page of this entertaining book. What makes Eamon Kelly's marvellous humour especially sharp is that he is heir to a great oral tradition–*he is the Prince of Irish storytellers.*

IN IRELAND LONG AGO

Kevin Danaher

Those who have only the most hazy ideas about how our ancestors lived in Ireland will find enlightment in these essays which range widely over the field of Irish folklife . Kevin Danaher describes life in Ireland before the 'brave new world' crept into the quiet countryside. Or perhaps 'describes' is not the right word. He rather invites the reader to call on the elderly people at their homes, to listen to their tales and gossip and taste their food and drink; to step outside and marvel at their pots and pans, plough and flails; to meet a water diviner; to join a fraction fight; hurry to a wedding and bow down in remembrance of the dead.

In this book Kevin Danaher has not only given us a well balanced picture of life in Ireland, but has also gone far to capture the magic of the written word.

IN MY FATHER'S TIME

Eamon Kelly

In My Father's Time invites us to a night of storytelling by Ireland's greatest and best loved seanchaí, Eamon Kelly. The fascinating stories reveal many aspects of Irish life and character. There are tales of country customs; matchmaking, courting, love; marriage and the dowry system; emigration, American wakes and returned emigrants. The stream of anecdotes never runs dry and the humour sparkles and illuminates the stories.

Nowadays we find it hard to visualise the long dark evenings of times gone by when there was no electric light, radio or T.V. We find it even harder to realise that such evenings were not long enough for the games, singing, music, dancing and storytelling that went on.